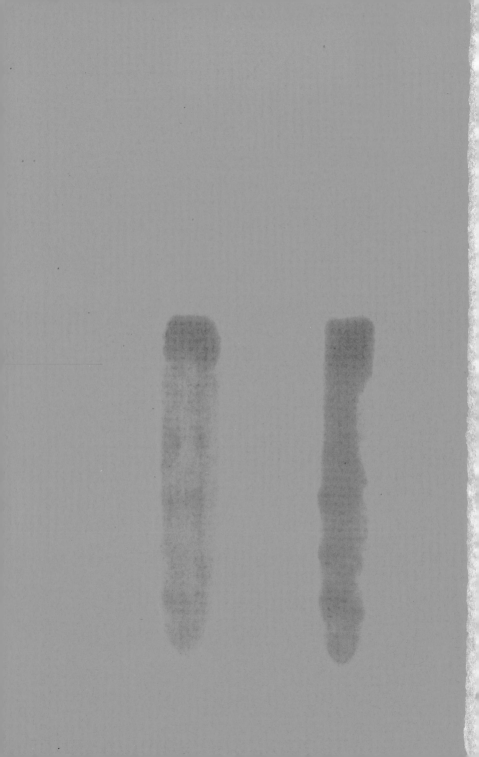

Out
of Time

A CHARLOTTE ZOLOTOW BOOK

Out
of Time

Stories Compiled by
Aidan Chambers

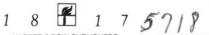

1 8 1 7 5718

HARPER & ROW, PUBLISHERS

Cambridge, Philadelphia, San Francisco, London, Mexico City, São Paolo, Singapore, Sydney

NEW YORK

Out of Time
Copyright © 1984 by Aidan Chambers
The Blades © 1984 by Joan Aiken Enterprises Ltd
Hally's Paradise © 1984 by Douglas Hill
Zone of Silence © 1984 by Monica Hughes
Songs from the Galaxy: Extinction is Forever, Rigel Light © 1984 by Louise Lawrence
In a Ship Called Darkness 3 © 1984 by Christopher Leach
Captain Courage and the Rose Street Gang © 1984 by Jan Mark
Pied Piper © 1984 by Ann Ruffell
Program Loop © 1984 by Jill Paton Walsh
Urn Burial © 1984 by Robert Westall
First published in Great Britain by The Bodley Head Ltd, London

Library of Congress Cataloging in Publication Data
Main entry under title:
Out of time.

"A Charlotte Zolotow book."
Summary: A collection of ten futuristic stories by
writers of young adult fiction, including Robert
Westall and Joan Aiken.
1. Science fiction, English. 2. Short stories,
English. [1. Science fiction. 2. Short stories]
I. Chambers, Aidan.
PZ5.09354 1985   [Fic]   85-42631
ISBN 0-06-021201-2
ISBN 0-06-021202-0 (lib. bdg.)

Contents

Songs from the Galaxy
1. Extinction Is Forever

LOUISE LAWRENCE

Vanya stared across the vast ruins of a civilization, devastated miles of tumbled concrete, twisted girders and the blackened remains of walls. It was nothing to do with the vengeance of God, Kermondley said. It was the result of a nuclear holocaust. All her life Vanya had known about the holocaust and many times she had played among the ruins of towns and cities on the edge of the lifeless land. But this time it was different or maybe she was different . . . older and more understanding. She had listened to Kermondley teaching history as once she had listened to the sea-wives telling fairy tales but now, suddenly, it all became real and she sensed the almighty meaning.

The Ancients were not simply a legendary race, just marble statues in the sea-museums, cold carved forms of men and women, artworks and artifacts and strange-sounding names. Rodin and Renoir and Richard Burton had really existed, as real and alive as she was now. Here, where the wind mourned and sighed across a loneliness of bones and dust, had been a city full of people.

"They called themselves *Homo sapiens,*" Kermondley said. "Who can tell me the meaning of *Homo sapiens*?"

"Wise man?" someone said.

Kermondley nodded.

"They were joking, of course."

The students laughed.

Everyone knew that the Ancients had engineered their own extinction. Such appalling termination was nothing to laugh at, Vanya thought. Even Kermondley showed no respect for history, no reverence for his ancestors, no grief for the various millions of life forms that had been lost. What Vanya felt was a terrible pity for the stupidity of *Homo sapiens*. But all around the laughter rose like mockery, shrill as the cries of extinct birds drifting inland from the shore, carried by the wind toward the silence.

Steven moved among the wreckage of the Third World War. The dial on his time-machine had stopped midway through the thirty-first century and time on his wristwatch showed a quarter past noon. Two hours ago it had been 1995 and himself a student of physics at the University of London, watching the peace campaigners marching to Trafalgar Square.

"Are they right to demand the abolition of nuclear weapons?" Professor Goddard had murmured. "Or is it, as the government claims, only the threat of nuclear war that guarantees world peace?"

Steven shrugged, loaded the video-camera.

It took proof, not opinions, to convince governments.

"I'll bring back a film of the end of the world," he had promised.

"I prefer to hope you will film the future of the human race," the old professor had replied.

But that had been in 1995.

Then it was still possible to hope.

It was even possible to believe the human race had a future.

But Steven had seen them commit the unforgivable act. He had seen the white clouds mushroom over England and the black ash falling on the land. He had witnessed the whimpering aftermath of the war they said would never happen, the hell of human dying and genetic decline. What new life was born sickened and failed . . . plant, animal and human. It seemed that nothing survived. After a thousand years there was only ruins and silence, the moan of the wind and the wash of the waves against the shore. What Steven had on film was proof of destruction, desolation without hope. But suddenly, far away and strangely incongruous . . . he heard laughter.

"Don't laugh at them!" Vanya cried.

It was an odd thing to say, an odd reaction . . . as if she believed the Ancients listened, a city full of ghostly souls made vulnerable by genocide and shame. There were tears in her eyes as she turned away. And then Kermondley understood . . . Vanya had realized that history had really happened and all his years of teaching were suddenly worthwhile.

He watched her swim toward the shore, the line of wharfs and rusting wrecks of ships and fallen warehouses. He saw her reach the flight of crumbled steps, her webbed hands heaving herself up in one lithe arching motion of water and light, reflections of sky on wet scales.

"Where's she going?" someone asked him.

"Do we follow?" asked another.

Kermondley shook his head.

He remembered himself at Vanya's age. He remembered the moment when history had come alive for him too. In another city, just like this one, he had felt the anguish of the Ancients dying, heard the scream of unborn generations echoing through time. He too had been felled by feelings of horror and grief. But now Kermondley could laugh at the arrogance of those who had called themselves wise . . . for his kind had been formed among the ashes of their world and he was glad they had not survived.

Steven walked toward the sound of distant voices, his footsteps silent in the dust. He came to water and acres of drowned streets, a great river estuary where Thames-side London had been. In a stench of seaweed and barnacles he saw her haul herself onto the land. He realized then that she was human . . . or had been.

He closed his eyes, leaned against the vitrified remains of a doorpost, waited for the horror and repulsion to subside and his thoughts to become rational. He should have expected it. He should have known if anything survived the holocaust it was bound to be a mutation. He remembered the banners the peace campaigners had carried . . . EXTINCTION IS FOREVER, they said.

And maybe it was not enough to build a time-machine, not enough to present the governments of the world with evidence of genocide. Maybe it would not persuade them to disarm. And simply by establishing their nuclear arsenals they had already accepted the possibility that untold millions of people would die. The public too had already accepted it. Mass destruction was a box-office hit. Earthquakes, infernos, nuclear war itself was being shown in every local cinema. People actually paid to watch it!

Sometimes Steven believed that the human race was willing its own annihilation, that it was a suicide instinct triggered naturally whenever the species put too great a strain upon the environment. Rabbits failed to breed . . . lemmings flung themselves from a cliff and drowned in the sea . . . and human beings went to war. It was a biological fail-safe, a way of preserving the species by reducing the number of individuals. But this time they would go too far.

Extinction was forever.

But maybe if they knew what they would become . . .

Steven raised the video-camera. This was the hope Professor Goddard had asked for. This was the future of the human race, a true daughter of the holocaust . . . a scaly mutant, mackerel-colored, sea-dwelling. And out in the estuary a whole shoal of them!

Vanya let the dry dust trickle through her fingers. The past belonged to her and all that once lived was as real and precious as she was now. She saw a sungleam break through the clouds, gold light touching the crumbled heart of the city, making it sacred. The stillness was so intense she was almost afraid. Out in the estuary the swimmers turned toward the distant beach. Vanya was tempted to rejoin them but something moved within the darkness of a broken doorway. Something emerged from the shadows and became a man.

Homo sapiens was not extinct!

The camera whirred and clicked.

And Vanya's voice was a scream across the open water.

"Kermondley! Come back!"

Steven gaped at her.

Her voice was beautiful, clear as a bell or a bird call, a sonar echo or a siren's song . . . each word pure and distinct in perfect English. She was not some kind of human subspecies. She was a being in her own right who perceived and communicated and was aware. Her bright aquamarine eyes regarded him nervously, her curiosity tinged with fear.

"I won't hurt you," Steven assured her.

One webbed finger pointed to the camera.

"You carry a weapon!" she said.

"It's a video-machine," he corrected.

"You used to kill," she said. "All the Ancients did. They killed everything that lived upon the land . . . including themselves."

"Hell!" said Steven. "Is that all that has survived of us . . . our blasted murderous reputation?"

Kermondley would never know what caused him to look back. Perhaps unconsciously he heard her cry or sensed her fear. For a while he could see nothing but the dazzle of light on water and waves swilling around the broken dome of St. Paul's cathedral. But then on the skyline of land he saw that Vanya was not alone. Someone was with her, framed in a sunlit doorway . . . the dark silhouette of a man.

Kermondley blinked.

He was reminded of the small bronze statuette he had dredged from the silt of sunken towns around Southampton water. But this was no museum piece. This man was alive . . . a figure that moved as Vanya moved, approached as she retreated, paused and raised his hands in the age-old gesture of peace or surrender.

Above the drowned spans of antique bridges Kermondley trod water and could not believe his eyes. The Ancients had become extinct a thousand years ago . . . like dodos and mastodons they were gone from the world. World-over the land had decayed to deserts of dust, supported no life larger than lizards and sand-flies and forests of sparse vegetation that clung to the rivers' reaches. Not even birds had survived. Yet Kermondley saw a man.

He called the students back.

"Tell me I'm dreaming," Kermondley said.

They looked at him, puzzled.

"Over on the shore where Vanya is . . . what do you see?" Kermondley asked them. "What do you make of that shape in the doorway that looks to me like a man?"

"Everything died of radiation," Vanya said. "But the oceans diffused it and the seas contained our only source of food. So we had to adapt and become aquatic. We had to hunt the shoals of fish hundreds of miles from the nearest shore, and cultivate seaweed. . . ."

Steven stared at her.

It was not mutation she talked of.

It was evolution.

Natural selection, which should have taken millions of years, had created a different species within a few generations. Men had to swim for survival . . . their skin turning to scales, feet to flippers. Now, looking at Vanya, not much remained of her human ancestry . . . just her voice, her aquamarine eyes and the pale breasts that made her female.

"Do you breed underwater?" he asked her.

Vanya felt embarrassed.

The way Steven looked at her, the way he questioned her . . . it was as if he regarded her as some kind of biological specimen, as if sea-people were no different from dolphins or seals. Maybe he imagined her among a colony, hauled up like sea-cows on a barren beach to wait for the breeding season. He did not seem to realize . . .

"There are cities under the sea," she said primly.

"Half of London by the look of it," Steven said.

"Not ruins!" said Vanya. "Living cities! Pressurized domes full of warmth and light! Sea gardens bloom beyond our windows in colors like the land has never known. We have music and drama, museums and galleries and schools of learning. Under the sea we eat and sleep and, yes, we breed."

An underwater civilization!

Incredulity showed on Steven's face, turned to nervousness as he saw Kermondley re-crossing the estuary, his dark shape speeding through the water followed by a dozen more. Suddenly Steven realized that *he* was the alien, the intruder, out of place and out of time. And if the sea-people could build cities under the ocean they were even more accomplished than the human race, more advanced, more intelligent . . . maybe more dangerous.

Muscles rippled, flashed and shone with blue-green sheen as Kermondley gained the lower steps and started to climb. Steven backed away. Stones from a wall slipped and fell as he knocked against it and the video-camera hung heavy and useless around his neck. He wished he had brought a gun, or a harpoon . . . something to defend himself with . . . anything. His fingers gripped a jagged lump of concrete as the rest of the sea-people crowded onto the land.

"Stay right where you are!" Steven howled.

Vanya laughed.

"We're all quite harmless," she said. "It's only the history class and Kermondley who teaches us. He always said history was alive but I bet he never expected to meet a real live *Homo sapiens* who should have been extinct!"

Kermondley stopped, not because he was afraid of being struck by a lump of concrete but because he sensed the Ancient was afraid. He probably recognized the sea-people as aquatic descendants of his own race and expected them to display the same mistrust, the same tendency to attack first and ask questions afterward. He motioned the students to stay behind him, waited as Vanya laughed her reassurances, then bowed his head in greeting. Not by the flicker of an eyelid did Kermondley betray his own, more terrible fear.

"Be welcome, *Homo sapiens*," Kermondley said.

"His name's Steven," said Vanya.

"And we were hardly wise," Steven admitted.

Kermondley smiled.

"It's a little late to realize that, my friend."

"Not where I come from," Steven said.

"Space?" Kermondley said hopefully.

"Time," said Steven. "1995."

Kermondley nodded.

His fear was established now.

"I thought perhaps you had returned from the stars," Kermondley said. "A space traveler cryogenically frozen for ten centuries. I didn't know the Ancients actually invented a machine that could travel time."

"Officially we haven't," Steven told him.

"But unofficially you have?" Kermondley prompted.

It was Steven's turn to smile.

Apart from himself no one knew they had invented a time-machine, either officially or unofficially. Even Professor Goddard waiting in the laboratory could not know until Steven returned. Government departments, heads of the armed services and scientists all over the world waited with bated breaths. Should time travel become a proven reality, its effects on the past and future of the human race seemed virtually unlimited.

"This is our first experiment," Steven said. "We needed to know what would happen in the future in order to prevent it. Many of us predicted it, of course, but now I have proof." He patted the video-camera. "Proof of the war and what happens afterward . . . you and Vanya and all of this."

Kermondley understood.

Steven's eyes said what his words did not, stared bitterly and fixedly out across the estuary to the fallen dome of the cathedral. He could not accept human extinction. He would return to his own time, present this evidence of the future, and the nuclear holocaust would never happen. The London Steven loved would rise again from the sea and all Kermondley's kind would never exist.

The thought touched Vanya too, triggered the same fear. She had always accepted the legacy of barren land and living ocean and never wished it could be different . . . but Steven did. Steven hated everything he saw because all he saw was the terrible ruins of his own world, his own civilization. He did not see Vanya's world . . . the green perpetual beauty and peace of the undersea cities. He did not understand how good it was to be alive in the present time. He just wanted it gone . . . everything restored to what it was. Steven was trying to change the future and it did not occur to him that his future was Vanya's past.

"History is a living process," Kermondley had said.

Vanya could feel it.

History contained inside herself.

For her the universe had formed and spread. For her the Earth revolved around the sun and life evolved. She was the reason why countless millions of species had become extinct. She was the reason why the Ancients had dropped their bombs and died over decades of terror and pain. The whole of history had happened that she might exist.

"And no one can change it," Vanya thought. "No one can change history!"

But maybe Steven could.

Across the dusty space of land she met Kermondley's gaze, teacher and pupil in a moment of recognition. The thought was the same in both of them. But she was the only one on the landward side, the only one who could act. Vanya hesitated, appalled by the awfulness of what she must do. But Kermondley's eyes urged her, willed her to go. She turned away, searched for Steven's footprints in the dust and followed them into the city.

Steven squatted on his heels on the cliff edge of the street, watching the water swill against the old foundations, a slow relentless erosion. The ebb tide left its line of green weed on the dome of St. Paul's and sea voices whispered around him, alien, inhuman, Kermondley's students crowding the steps, restless and waiting. Steven had been in their time for less than half an hour and already he had seen all he wanted to see and was ready to go. The loneliness depressed him, the immense absence of everything he knew. The silence grated on his nerves.

He had no reason to stay in this godforsaken future any longer but Kermondley delayed him.

"This being a history lesson," Kermondley said, "we would like to take this unique opportunity. . . . would you mind?"

"Sure," said Steven. "What can I tell you?"

"What was it really like in 1995?" one of the students asked.

They had no idea.

They could not even imagine trees in St. James's Park or Christmas lights glittering along Oxford Street. They had never tasted chestnuts or potato chips or strawberries and cream. They had never smelled roses, touched cat's fur, heard a blackbird sing, ridden the fun-fair rides or the rush-hour train. All the things Steven took for granted were meaningless to them.

Surrounded by ocean and empty lands Kermondley's students could grasp very little of everyday human existence. It was like trying to describe colors to people born blind, or spinning them fairy tales. They had thought all Ancients were violent, that everyone went around attacking everyone else . . . that tanks and guns and atom bombs were personal possessions. It was not easy to convince them that most Ancients had not wanted war.

"If no one wanted it how come it happened?" they asked him.

"Maybe it won't," he said.

"It already has," said Kermondley.

"Not in my time," said Steven. "In 1995 we can still

prevent it and my evidence will make the vital difference. Now I must go. It's been nice meeting you."

He turned toward the ruins of the city.

Vanya stood in the broken doorway.

Sea-green tears shimmered in her eyes.

"I'll wait for you, Steven," Vanya said.

And he thought she was crazy.

No one waited for a thousand years!

The future was dependent on the past.

If anyone should change the past . . .

"We had to make sure," Kermondley said.

"There was nothing he could have done," said Vanya. "We know that! We're here! If he had succeeded we wouldn't exist!"

"We had to make sure," Kermondley repeated.

"One nuclear war guaranteed!" Vanya said bitterly.

"The Ancients still have a choice," Kermondley reminded her.

"Steven doesn't," she said dully.

Kermondley sighed.

"At least he's alive."

But Vanya knew that being alive would be no consolation to Steven. Heavy on her conscience was the sick knowledge of what she had done to him. She followed Kermondley down the steps. Her skin felt itchy and dry. She needed the silk sweet water to wash the dust from her scales. She needed to swim away, far out to sea, and forget.

Her fellow students waited and called.

"Hurry up, Vanya!"

"It's way past lunchtime!"

"And Kermondley said we can go!"

"We'll race you to the restaurant!"

"Are you coming?"

"You go," Kermondley said quietly. "I'll wait for Steven."

Vanya shook her head.

She too would wait.

And his cry rose from the heart of the ruined city making a pain in her heart like she had never known before. It was a cry of anguish and despair that went on and on, a terrible human sound. Vanya sobbed inconsolably knowing what he had found. She had smashed the workings of his time-machine. He was trapped here now for the rest of his life . . . *Homo sapiens* on the verge of extinction, the only one of his kind.

Professor Goddard switched off the laboratory light and closed the door. He had waited all afternoon and evening but Steven had not come back. The experiment had failed. His theory of time travel remained unproven and a young man was missing, presumed dead.

Professor Goddard sighed and shook his head. It was not only guilt that troubled him. He also knew the consequences of academic failure. He would not get a second chance to build a time-machine. His research grant would not be renewed and he would have to accept retirement from the university, an old discredited scientist exiled to a bungalow in Bognor Regis . . . growing zinnias perhaps.

He sighed again, buttoned his jacket and went out into the night. He was just one more old man whose life had not amounted to very much. He did not read the writing on the banner that someone had tied to the front railings.

EXTINCTION IS FOREVER, it said.

2. Rigel Light

LOUISE LAWRENCE

Rigel is the brightest star in the constellation of Orion, a vast blue binary sun with planets revolving around it . . . and on the third planet of its solar system Maggie was born. Her home was an isolated farming complex in the foothills of the Indigo Mountains where Jessica, her mother, worked as a bio-technician along with Ed Barnes and the others who shared the communal living quarters. They were employed by the Galactic Mining Company to produce Earth-type foods for the various mining settlements scattered around the planet.

Humid and forested, plagued by electrical storms and only partially explored, Rigel Three was hardly suitable for colonization. But it was rich in minerals and metal ores and the Mining Company paid high wages to anyone willing to work there. They even accepted Jessica, large with child in the months before Maggie was born, although they provided no facilities for children. Her nursery had been the acres of glass-houses and the open fields of soya beans, sweet corn and cabbage. And baby-minders varied with the duty rota . . . Brian or Sarah, Ritchie or Sue or, best of all, Ed Barnes.

From the moment Maggie could toddle she latched onto Ed. He was a rough Australian and called her the nipper. He gave her shoulder rides, told her fairy stories, answered her questions and dandled her on his knee. He watched her grow, the only youngster among half a dozen adults who had neither the time nor the inclination to pay her much attention. And the native field hands were born without vocal cords, speechless menials who were not much company for a human child. Left to her own devices Maggie chattered to herself, invented solitary games, ran wild and unsupervised under the blue heat of the sun. And once, when the gates were opened and the produce truck left for the nearest mining settlement, she went exploring.

Her child's mind admitted no fear among the great dark trees beyond the perimeter fences. The jungle sang to her with its unseen choirs of insects and birds, a world of blue diffuse light and sapphire shadows. She climbed toward the high silence of the hills, to the sacred burial grounds where the spirits lived that ate the bodies of the native dead. And there, across the final openness where the jungle ended and the mountains rose toward the sky, she saw the flame people dancing. Spellbound, Maggie watched them, living forms that were veiled in tongues of pale fire. And the landscape shimmered around her in indescribable shades of mauve and violet with the forest growing inky behind her as the great sun set. Long shadows fell across the blue-grass ridges.

There were voices then, human voices howling for her to come home, transmitting their terror. Beautiful and dancing the flame people came drifting toward her but Maggie screamed and fled. She tried to tell Ed . . . fire fairies, she said. But he spanked her around the legs and Jessica sent her to bed.

"Don't ever go outside the gates again!" Jessica said.

As Maggie grew older she forgot about the flame people. There were other things to occupy her mind. Even on outback planets education was compulsory. During the evening darkness, when colors were strange and harsh beneath the yellow inside lights, Jessica and Ritchie taught her to read and write and Brian taught her basic mathematics. Later the video-machine took over. For hours each day she was locked inside with its flickering screen as the strawberries flowered and the bean fields smelled sweet at the start of the short dry summer season. Rigelian field hands moved among the raspberry canes, their pale young faces streaked with dirt and sweat. Mute and motherless and little more than children, they lived for only seven years and worked from dawn to dusk for no wages. But to Maggie they retained a freedom she had lost and sometimes she wished she had been born Rigelian.

"You've got to stay inside and learn!" Ed Barnes told her.

But more often than not Maggie was gone . . . a barefooted girl, willful and undisciplined, hiding among acres of blossoming beans. She ate strawberries and carrots and raw peas, whatever crop was in season, and did not return until twilight.

Then the fear began for those who had come from Earth. The fence wires hummed and sparked with high voltage electricity and pale points of fire flickered across the lower slopes of the Indigo Mountains. They were the Rigel Lights, Ed told her . . . will-o'-the-wisps or Saint Elmo's fires. And down in the graveyard by the pumpkin patch five men were buried who had died from the madness those lights made. They get inside your head, Ed said. But the fences kept them out and it was never Maggie's fear.

For her the Rigel Lights were always beautiful. She could watch them for hours, delicate and dancing, rainbow spots of color in the midnight blue distance coming nearer and nearer. It never occurred to her they might attack. But Brian talked of ghouls and Sarah feared them and many a time Jessica came screaming across the darkening fields to haul Maggie back inside.

"How many times do I have to tell you!" Jessica shouted. "When you see those things around you're to stay in the house!"

"That kid wants taking in hand," Ed said.

"Someone to keep a permanent eye on her," said Sarah.

"Yesterday," said Ritchie, "I caught her fiddling with the gate controls. And someone turned the sprinklers on full in number three glass-house."

"I don't have eyes in the back of my head!" Jessica said.

"She'll grow up to be educationally backward," said Sue. "That's three times this week she's dodged lessons. You're going to have to get a minder for her."

"Those Rigelians give me the creeps!" Jessica said.

"But we're thinking of Maggie, not you," said Ed.

Maggie watched him hatch from the egg, a vague pink shape the size of a human baby. A month before, when she had come with Ed to order him, the sensors had sexed him as female. But the newly emerged mind made its own decision. Fluid and sticky, the shape budded arms and legs and male appendages and Maggie watched in total fascination until Jessica caught her hand and pulled her away.

"We ordered a female," Jessica said primly.

"Mistakes do happen," said the incubation assistant.

"Do you have another?" Jessica asked.

"I don't want another!" Maggie wailed. "I want that one! It was my egg he came out of! I chose it! Ed said I could!"

"And there are no others," said the incubation assistant.

Jessica glanced around the hatchery.

There must have been hundreds.

Rigelians failed to breed in captivity, failed even to reach sexual maturity during their short seven years of life. The eggs were laid by wild Rigelians, great abandoned clutches in remote parts of the planet that were carefully culled and brought to the hatchery. Everywhere in the battery-heated cots the white shells cracked and split under the hot lights, poured out their pink amorphous blobs of life.

It was the first time Jessica had visited the hatchery . . . the first time she had witnessed the birth of these alien things. Hard to believe that in three months' time these shapeless maggoty babies would be fully grown into the black-haired child-people of Rigel Three, ready to work in the fields or down the mines, replacing those who were due to die in the autumn. And hard to believe that the changeling boy whom Jessica was so loath to accept would become a minder for her own daughter.

"The psycho-emotional read-outs show no distinction between the Rigelian sexes," the incubation assistant informed her. "I can assure you that after undergoing the statutory training the boy will prove perfectly suitable."

"And I do want him!" Maggie sobbed. "Ed said he was mine!"

Jessica sighed.

She returned to lean above the cot and the coal-black eyes of the alien child seemed to fix on her face. They saw too much, understood too much, and she feared the silence of the mind behind them. The blackness glittered and Jessica shuddered. After eight years she ought to be used to it . . . the eerie haunted atmosphere of the blue planet . . . those black Rigelian eyes and dumb silences . . . but she knew she would never feel easy with him around the house. But Maggie wept for him, wanted him, a pink baby thing, newborn and defenseless. Maggie did not understand . . . a few hours from now he would clutch his first fruit and feed himself . . . and tomorrow he would take his first step.

Yet for Maggie's sake Jessica was bound to own him.
She bent to comfort.

"What will you call him?" she asked.

Before Maggie left the hatchery she named him Kirk,
after the starship captain on an antique video-show. He
was delivered to the farming complex a week before the
autumn rains began along with the replacement field
hands. Like them he was tall and bony with black curling
hair and smouldering eyes. On the human age scale he
looked maybe fifteen years old and eight-year-old Maggie
gazed at him in awe. He was not as she expected, not
the Kirk of her imagination who had shared her life these
past weeks and become her friend. He was dour and
silent . . . a total stranger. Disappointment and anger
mixed with Maggie's shyness and she clung to Ed's hand
whilst Sarah showed him around.

He would sleep with the field hands in the outside cha-
lets but the rest of the time he would spend with Maggie
and take his meals in the communal kitchen . . . like
one of the family, Sarah said. And video-lessons, Sarah
informed him, lasted from 0900 hours to 1630 and supper
was served at 1815. He was to ensure that Maggie appeared regularly for both.

Kirk nodded his head in understanding. Like the rest
of his kind his obedience was perfect and there was no
question of anyone not trusting him. He had been taught
to fear the Rigel Lights as much as humans did and
Brian showed him how to operate the gate controls and
switch on the voltage if under attack. He was also
given the key to the video-room and a whistle to summon

help in case of fire, or accident, or trouble with Maggie.

"And that's all there is to it," Sarah said.

"We hope you'll be happy here," said Brian.

Ed rested his hand on Kirk's shoulder.

"We're not expecting miracles," Ed said. "Just do your best, son, that's all we ask. And you behave yourself!" he said to Maggie.

Deep inside the resentment began.

And everyone watched to see what Kirk would do and how she reacted. He spelled out his message in simple sign language which Maggie could not fail to understand and held out his hand for her to accompany him into the video-room. On the blind side of Ed Maggie stuck out her tongue. Nothing showed on Kirk's face, no anger, no response . . . but his dark eyes seemed to bore into her brain, a compelling blackness from which she could not look away. It was as if he touched her deep inside, soft and fluttering, sifting through every nerve in her body, searching for something and finding nothing but hostility. He understood and the blackness glittered as he pointed to the door a second time, then clenched his fist to show that something very nasty might happen to her if she did not obey.

Ed laughed.

Rigelians were nonaggressive.

But Kirk had been trained to use human gestures.

And he needed human support.

"Best do what he says, little lady," Ed said.

"Unless you want a tanned backside," said Sarah.

Maggie went, muttering in her mind, mean nasty feelings simmering below the surface. They were all on Kirk's side

now . . . even Ed . . . and there was no one left for
Maggie. It was his fault. She would make him sorry he
had ever come here! She would make him wish he had
never hatched from the egg!

Maggie set out to be deliberately difficult, a bane to
Kirk in every possible way. She knew the rules about not
touching the video-controls but she altered them all and
put the blame on him. Colors pulsed in lurid green and
purple. Voices gabbled, jammed at full speed and the
computer link-up broke. It took Brian three days to fix it
and Kirk bore the brunt of his temper. Then, twice in
one day, Maggie had him unlock the video-room door
for her to use the lavatory only to run away. It was uncanny how quickly he found where she was hiding but
there was no way he could make her return to the house
units without using physical force. All he could do was
blow the emergency whistle and wait for someone to
come.

"My patience is beginning to wear very thin," Jessica
said.

Then the rains began.

And the field hands started to sicken.

Ritchie, who was the base medic, could do nothing
to save them. Nine died within a week and during that
week, as if they were attracted by the scent of death,
the Rigel Lights attacked. All night Maggie watched them,
bolts of rainbow fire that hurled themselves at the fence
wire only to recoil and try again, or explode in a shower
of colored sparks. Laser beams blasted away the darkness
as Ed and Brian fought. Jessica, savage with fear, used a

primitive flame gun and Sue worked on the back-up generator to boost the fluctuating power.

And all the while the rain poured down.

It rained for three successive days and nights and for three successive nights the Rigel Lights attacked. But finally, when the last field hand died, they went away . . . diminished into distance until they appeared no more than fallen stars twinkling against the blue-velvet backdrop of the mountains. In a sodden dawn the burial parties toiled up the jungle track to the sacred burial grounds.

Kirk bent his head as they passed.

It was his first experience of death.

Bodies being buried in black earth.

"The worms eat them," Maggie told him. "And Ritchie says the Rigel Lights feed off all the smelly gases. And that's what will happen to you in seven years' time." And she saw in the black depths of his eyes a little flicker of fear.

Autumn was never an easy time at the farming complex. The Rigelian deaths left their mark, their losses felt even in human hearts after a seven-year acquaintance. The new field hands had yet to learn the routine and the weather alternated between breathless heat and violent thunderstorms. Number five glass-house shattered in a freak wind and a thousand young cabbage plants were washed from the ground. Human tempers frayed around the edges. They seemed to move in a miasma of mud and dampness, a blue gloom, sodden and inescapable. And this was the time Maggie chose to be difficult. This was the time she forced Kirk to blow his whistle . . . again and again and again. Tramping down through two fields of battered blueberry bushes Jessica blew her top.

"I'm sick of you two!" Jessica screamed. "There's an ore freighter leaving next month," she said to Maggie. "And you're going to be on it! You can go to boarding school back on Earth! And as for you," she said to Kirk. "For all the use you are as a child-minder you might as well go join the field hands! Now both of you . . . clear off back to the video-room!"

All the way back to the house units Jessica's words howled in Maggie's head, a tirade of anger that went on and on. And the spaceship to Earth was the ultimate threat, the ultimate rejection. And maybe Kirk sensed the fear she felt for he held out his hand as if to touch her, a gesture of compassion in the silence. But it was he who had blown the whistle. It was his fault Jessica would send her away, billions of miles to an unknown Earth. Her face twisted in a monstrous anger and she kicked him hard on the shin.

It was as if something struck her, a slap inside her head that sent her reeling. She fell against the opposite wall, cowered in the corner by the video-machine and covered her head with her arms to try and ward off the blows. But the pain went on . . . the cuff of Kirk's hand against her mind as his voice battered her.

"Stupid! Vicious! Ignorant Maggie! What good has it done you? What have you gained from tormenting me? Nothing! You're alone like you never were before! And how does it feel to be hurt, and hated and not wanted?

How do you think I've felt? Now you pay for it, Maggie!"

"No!" Maggie whimpered. "Not anymore! Don't hit me anymore!"

The hurting stopped.

"We could have been friends," Kirk said. "Both of us together. I came here for you. I wanted to like you." He gripped her wrists. "It's not too late," he said. "If we work together . . . if we make up for these past weeks your mother might not send you away. You've got to try, Maggie. You can't grow up to be stupid and mindless and vicious. Don't you want to learn about the world you came from? Don't you want to learn about plants and stars and chemistry?"

Maggie stared at him.

Soft black eyes seen blurred through her tears.

"You can talk!" she said wonderingly.

"No . . . you can listen," he said.

And she realized then that his voice was silent.

That she heard him only in her heart and in her head.

Jessica did not send Maggie away on the Earth-bound freighter, nor was Kirk sent from the house to join the field hands. Suddenly they began to work together. And not only did they run through the scheduled video-lessons . . . they also began to use the micro-library stored in the computer. Learning absorbed them and they troubled no one. But Ed sensed the strange affinity that lay between them . . . companions in adversity and more than that . . . with Maggie Kirk no longer used sign language. Indeed it was almost uncanny the way Maggie interpreted his dumbness, the way she laughed and spoke to him and even argued . . . as if the silence brimmed with the unheard things he said. Ed was convinced Kirk talked to her.

"You mean telepathic communication?" Ritchie said.

"It wouldn't surprise me where Rigelians are concerned," said Sue. "But Maggie's human."

"She's a nipper," said Ed. "Nippers have strange ways of knowing."

"If it's true," said Ritchie. "And Kirk is communicating with her. . . . Jessica's not going to like it."

"Do we have to tell her?" Ed said. "Where's the harm in it, I say? They're both of them nippers and Maggie needs a friend."

"We don't *have* to tell her," Ritchie said dubiously.

"And there are none so blind as those who will not see," said Sue. "Jessica will come around to it in her own sweet time without any help from us."

So the years passed.

During the two following autumns when the field hands died the Rigel Lights attacked again . . . but then, for some unknown reason, they withdrew altogether from the nearby ridges, drifting so far away among the mountains that even the fear of them was gone. Humans slept easy in their beds and during the day the gates were left open. For the first time in her life Maggie was free to come and go. And Jessica saw only what she wanted to see . . . an ordinary little girl with Kirk in charge of her, skipping beside him up the jungle track . . . a child chasing butterflies across the sacred burial grounds or paddling in pools below cliffs that were purple as plums in the blue afternoon light.

Blue summer followed blue summer and Jessica never dreamed of what would come. Sometimes Maggie's intense enigmatic conversations with no one in particular puzzled her . . . and sometimes Kirk's eyes across the supper table scared her with their intimations of intelligence . . . but mostly Jessica failed to notice what Ed and Sue, Ritchie and Sarah, saw quite clearly and Brian automatically accepted. Brian had always known how deeply Kirk and Maggie were involved. In overall charge of the computer, he knew what video-lessons were being run through and had followed their development. It was as if they were searching for something . . . the meaning of existence perhaps.

"They're into quantum physics and applied theology now!" Brian said.

"Who are?" Jessica asked him.

"Maggie and Kirk," he said.

"Don't be absurd," said Jessica. "He's just a dumb Rigelian and she's no more than a child."

"Dumb?" said Brian. "He's about as dumb as Einstein was and Maggie's not far behind. We may credit Rigelians with no more than primitive intelligence but in this case we were wrong. And I don't know where you've been these last six years, Jessica, but at fourteen you can hardly call Maggie a child. She and Kirk are pretty close, you know. The original beautiful relationship, I'd say. Hadn't you noticed?"

Jessica stared at him.

She could not believe what he said.

She did not want to believe . . . but Brian nodded toward the window and she was bound to look. In the sapphire twilight Jessica saw them walking with Ed along the avenue of glass-houses . . . a girl on the threshold of womanhood and a young man with dark curling hair. She saw how they laughed at something Ed said, then smiled at each other. She saw how their hands touched and held. Jessica clenched her fists. The shock of realization turned into anger.

"How long has this been going on?" Jessica screamed.

The farmstead turned wild.

Kirk was banished from the house to live among the field hands and Maggie was sent to bed, forbidden ever to see him again. And finally Jessica turned on Ed.

"You knew all along, didn't you?" Jessica shouted.

"Maybe I did," said Ed. "But it was always too late."

"What do you mean . . . too late?" Jessica said savagely. "He's a damned blasted alien, Ed! What the hell are you thinking of?"

"I'm thinking they love each other," Ed said quietly. "And I'm thinking there's nothing you, or I, or anyone else can do about it because in six months' time he'll be dead."

Pumpkin flowers bloomed palely in the blue dawn light and the human graveyard was white with starry blossoms. Maggie was not unaware of the irony of the place, the carved headstones symbolizing death in the midst of burgeoning life. Rain dripped from the overhead trees and

Kirk leaned against the picket fence and brooded. His shirt was soaked, as if he had been standing there all night.

"Jessica sent me," Maggie said. "You're to come to the house for breakfast, she says."

"Last night," said Kirk, "she told me never to darken her doors again!"

"And now she's prepared to apologize," said Maggie.

Kirk's voice came mocking into her mind.

"Apologize to a slave? That's big of her."

"You're not a slave!" Maggie objected.

"Don't be naive," he replied. "All Rigelians are slaves. We accepted that long ago so why deny it now?"

"Ed made it all right for us anyway," Maggie muttered.

"I suppose he pointed out that she need only turn a blind eye for another six months before I do her a favor and drop dead?" Kirk said.

"That's horrible!" Maggie said tearfully.

"It's true!" Kirk said bitterly. "We've run out of time, haven't we? Your mother should have stuck to what she said and made you stay away from me! Have you thought what it will be like for you, Maggie . . . watching me . . . waiting . . . knowing. I don't feel very brave. There's this godawful . . ."

He bit his lip.

Fear, Maggie thought.

He was afraid of death, the black termination, although he had always lived with the prospect just as she had done. But somehow it had always been in the future. Now the years had drained away and he stood on the edge of the last blue summer and finally faced it . . . the ultimate terror. And she stood beside him, equally afraid . . . afraid of the loneliness when he was gone, the terrible grief and a lifetime unbearable without him. She touched his arm, trying to comfort him but needing comfort herself.

He pointed to the gravestones.

"They were lucky," he said.

"They died of the Rigel Lights," said Maggie.

"But they didn't know they were going to," Kirk said. "They didn't know they would end when they had hardly begun to live. We've failed, Maggie. We've failed to find a meaning. Quantum physics or Wordsworth's poetry . . . it doesn't matter how many intimations of immortality we find. In the end the fear remains that there really is nothing. It's all been wasted, Maggie! I'm just a lump of worm meat . . . a source of methane for the Rigel Lights. Every breath I've taken has been totally and absolutely meaningless."

Maggie shook her head.

"You mean something to me," she said.

"And you won't be there," he said. "Not where I'm going."

"I will one day," she told him.

"Bones beside me in the black earth?" he asked.

Maggie shrugged.

"I want to be buried here," he said.

Toward the end of summer the Rigel Lights returned, lurked on the ridge above the farming complex as if they were waiting . . . death birds hovering on wings of fire, silent and menacing. Daylight dissolved them to a shimmer of heat devils dancing in the distance but every twilight they drew nearer, a flutter of rainbow fires among the trees exuding their eerie atmospheres. Maggie was always immune to the spooky feelings but they made the hairs stand up on the back of Brian's neck and sent cold shivers down Sarah's spine.

"What attracts them to us?" Jessica asked.

"Fear?" said Ritchie.

"Or the prospect of carrion?" said Brian.

"Me!" Kirk said silently.

"No!" said Maggie.

But his death was inevitable.

Autumn storms made a premature darkness . . . the sky growing inky above the Indigo Mountains. In sultry heat the rain sluiced down and five field hands sickened. Then it was Kirk's turn. All of a sudden he seemed gripped by an overwhelming lassitude and Maggie saw the spores in his skin start to sprout, branching mycelia of a mold that would finally cover him completely in a white cobwebby shroud and harden like bone.

Death came quickly for Rigelians, between one dawn and the next. But in the small stuffy chalet on the edge of the blueberry fields Kirk resisted it. Maggie could feel his fear in her heart, his screams in her head growing fainter and fainter. She tried to tear away the cobweb strands that covered his nose and mouth, the silken suffocating cocoon that Ritchie refused to surgically remove.

"It does no good," Sarah explained. "We've tried before and it's kinder to leave it."

"We can't just do nothing!" Maggie wept.

"Take her out of here," Ritchie told Sarah.

The woman's warm arms led her away.

Into a kind of madness.

She stood unmoving in the mud and rain, hearing the shriek of human voices, seeing the darkness pulse and flash with lights and laser beams. In a massed attack the flames battered the gates . . . blue into purple, crimson and emerald, rose-gold and brimstone yellow . . . desperate and dangerous. They get inside your head, Ed said . . . just like Kirk had gotten inside Maggie's. But this was a crazy babble . . . beings howling in anger and anguish, demanding to be let in.

The flame people!

Some latent memory flickered and died. Through a blur of tears or rain Maggie saw the stark silhouette of Sue, her hand reaching briefly toward the gate controls in the moment before she died . . . shot in the back by Brian's laser gun. And not only for Kirk did Maggie grieve in the soaking blue stillness of the following morning.

True to his wish Kirk was buried in the human graveyard next to Sue. Mud and rain of winter washed away the flowers and Maggie had never felt so alone. Her sense of loss was almost unbearable. Kirk was gone forever. She would never again hear his voice in her mind, feel his dark gaze touch her and his laughter spin through her veins. He had been so much a part of her she thought she was dying too.

Jessica was not devoid of understanding. She knew the hollow hopeless feelings left behind when some beloved person went for good, be it through death or desertion. It was the loss of Maggie's father that had brought Jessica to Rigel Three in the first place. And that was why she suggested Maggie should go . . . to Earth, with Brian who had terminated his contract with the Galactic Mining Company and would leave after serving out his notice.

"You have to think of your future," Jessica said.

"I reckon she's right there, girlie," Ed said kindly. "Time and distance will take away the pain, you see if it don't. And you can't stay here on this godforsaken planet for the rest of your life."

But Maggie had been born and brought up on that blue-drenched world. It was the only home she had ever known and everything she loved lay buried there. But with Kirk dead there was nothing to keep her . . . only a headstone in the graveyard carved with his name . . . only a memory that eluded her, scraps of knowledge that she failed to understand.

Daily in the blue spring rain when the jungle steamed with heat and the mountains were veiled in drifts of sapphire cloud, Maggie trekked down through the blueberry fields to stand by his grave. It was a compulsion that grew stronger as the days dried and drifted toward summer. Sometimes she would lean against the picket fence for hours without knowing why. A morbid preoccupation, Ritchie called it, and Jessica made the final arrangements for her departure.

"Maybe I don't want to go," Maggie said doubtfully.

"It's the best thing for you," Jessica said firmly. "The dead are dead and it does you no good to brood."

But it was not something dead Maggie sensed in the graveyard. It was something alive and sleeping, like a root tuber buried in earth. The spring rain disturbed it. The sunlight coaxed it awake. And Maggie waited for it to hatch from the soil . . . something other than flowers. Deep blue twilight settled over the land, an intense birdless silence broken only by Ed who came to fetch her for supper.

"I'm not hungry," Maggie said.

"Come back to the house units anyway," Ed said.

"Not yet," she replied.

"The Rigel Lights are about," Ed warned her.

"I know," said Maggie. "And they're only interested in the burying grounds, not me."

"You're not thinking of staying out here all night, are you?" Ed asked her.

"No," said Maggie. "Not all night." She gripped his arm. "It's starting to happen," she said. "Look over there."

Kirk . . . rest in peace, the headstone said.

And Ed was rooted to the spot.

He saw the earth heave up, split in a black crack. Fingers of fire licked at the edges of the open grave, and down inside a hellish blood-red light pulsed like a heartbeat, paused for a moment then poured itself out. Crumpled and shapeless, like a newly emerged butterfly, it lay inert on the ground, resting as the darkness deepened around it and Maggie held her breath. Ed's voice reached her as a cracked whisper.

"Run up to the house units and get my laser gun," Ed said.

"What for?" Maggie asked him.

"It's a blasted Rigel Light!" he said.

"It's not hurting *you*!" said Maggie.

"You know what they do!" Ed said urgently.

"They get inside your head," Maggie quoted.

"And they make you do things you didn't ought to do," said Ed. "Sue died because of them. Now go get that gun before the bloody thing moves!"

"It's not doing anything!" Maggie repeated. "And Sue died because Brian shot her!"

"She would have opened the gates!" said Ed.

And let them in, thought Maggie.

Flame people.

Finally she understood.

"And so did Sue," Maggie murmured. "She understood and had pity."

"What are you talking about?" Ed asked her.

"Flame people!" Maggie said. "Rigelians! That's what they are in their adult form . . . Rigel Lights. And we steal their eggs and use their children as slaves! And we let those children believe they will die at the end of seven years! They've hardly begun and we make them face termination. Think of it, Ed . . . all that fear . . . all those meaningless loveless childhoods! We don't hear them screaming but their parents do. If we are attacked by the Rigel Lights it's our own fault . . . a natural parental response . . . the desire to reach their children . . . to hold them, comfort them, teach. For them death isn't death, it's metamorphosis. And sometimes I'm ashamed I belong to the human race."

She turned on her heel and walked toward it . . .

A human girl and a Rigel Light . . .

A flame person, she said.

Ed's thoughts were reeling. It was all too much for him to take in . . . a life cycle that crossed the boundaries between mind and matter . . . beings of light, nebulous and insubstantial, who gave birth to eggs that hatched into flesh-and-blood children, who died and pupated and changed into light. Flame people . . . Ed could not believe it. He could not believe that shapeless blob of luminosity was sentient, capable of thought or feeling or compassion. He watched it rise . . . a pillar of silvery white brightness trailing its tongues of crimson fire. It was taller than he was . . . terrible, beautiful . . . an awesome powerful thing. He wanted to scream . . . "Come away from it Maggie!" . . . but she held out her hands to the crimson bright burning and her eyes shone with a strange kind of happiness.

"Hello Kirk," Maggie said. "Welcome back to my head."

Captain Courage
and the
Rose Street Gang

JAN MARK

Arty said, "I want to play in the street."

Arty's mother said, "For heaven's sake stop whining and get out from under my feet."

Arty squeezed past her, between the home laundry unit, where the week's washing was twirling in its drum, and the fast food module, into the leisure area. There was not very much more space in there, for his elder brother Lance was lying on the floor playing chess with PREM, his Programmed Response Module. PREM was an early model and had acquired a reciprocal twitch every time it extended its articulated limb to move a chess piece. Consequently it was continually backing away from the board, propelled in a leftward curve by the thrust of its single right arm. Lance, on his stomach, followed it around the room, pushing the chess board in front of him like a tray. He had been playing for only twenty minutes and he was already on his second circuit. PREM accelerated irritably. It was losing, and its programmed responses did not include good sportsmanship.

Arty said, "Lance, why don't we go and play in the street?"

"Too far," Lance said, shortly. "Anyway, it may be raining."

"I bet it's not."

"It may be by the time we get there."

Arty went to the Factcenter console and dialed Weatherdata; a map of southeast England appeared on the screen. Arty pressed the Locale key and the map dissolved into a close-up of Maidstone. He adjusted the volume control and a cheery voice chipped in: "Good morning, Dataseeker. The weather prospects in your area are good. Congratulations. This certainly looks like being a bright weekend for all you fortunate Maidstoneites. The forecast for today *and* tomorrow *and* Monday is bright sunshine and . . . and a party political broadcast on behalf of the Kent County Council and . . ."

Arty banged the tuning key.

". . . is bright sunshine and sunshine . . . retailing at ninety-five pounds with a discount . . ."

"Give it a kick," Lance advised. "Check."

". . . a slight breeze from the southwest should keep you comfortably cool. Thank you for calling. Have a nice day."

"There you are," Arty said. "It's not raining."

"I don't trust that thing," Lance said. "For all you know, that could be last week's forecast. No one's going to bother to find out, are they? They couldn't prove anything if they did. Look, I said check," he said to PREM. PREM put out its arm to remedy the situation and jittered backward under the storage unit.

"What's the point of being the Rose Street Gang if we never play in the street?" Arty complained. "We might just as well call ourselves the Walkway Mob or the Level Eleveners."

"And get mistaken for the Level Tenners? Not likely," Lance said. "Look, PREM, you're beaten. Why not give up? Anyway," he went on, "no one could say it." He experimented. "Leveleleveners . . . Leveleleveners . . . it sounds like a tongue-twister." He reached under the storage unit to winkle out his sulking robot.

"You said we could play in the street when summer came," Arty persisted.

"I don't feel like it," Lance said. "It's too much of a hassle getting there. Anyway, I'm going down to Beowulf's. He was getting a new hologram for his birthday. D'you want to come?"

"I suppose so. It doesn't look like we're going to do anything else, does it?"

Lance stowed PREM in the storage unit and they headed for the door.

"Where are you off to?" Mum yelled from the utility area, where the laundry module was spewing gray suds across the floor through faulty grommets.

"Just down to Beowulf's."

"What about lunch?"

"We'll be back for dinner."

"You'd better take these." Mum stepped across the

spreading puddle of scum and handed him a luncheon module full of anonymous plastic cubes. "You might as well finish them up," Mum said. "The labels have peeled off." The labels were also in the module, independently advertising the presence of Crunchy Haddock Bites, Crispy Banana Fries, Spicy Nibbles and Flaky Praties. The eatables from which they had disassociated themselves were all uniform six-centimeter blocks.

"You can have a sort of guessing game," Mum said, encouragingly. "You won't know which they are until you've tasted them."

Arty privately thought that without the labels they would not know what they were eating even after they'd eaten it. Sulking as obtrusively as PREM he followed his brother onto the walkway. In fact he had no objection at all to going to see Beowulf's hologram because he had heard, through rumor at the Education Center, that it was properly not a hologram at all, but one of the new autograms that operated without a plate. He had a hologram of his own, on which you could fight historic battles of the Second World War, but the machine, which had belonged to his father when *he* was a boy, was very nearly as historic as its subject matter, and the Germans kept winning at El Alamein. But at least it still worked.

He and Lance trudged in silence for about twenty minutes along the walkway, past Tesco's, Mothercare, the Education Center, which stretched for hundreds of meters, and the Hydroponic Memorial Facility where Senior Citizens dozed peacefully among the sandbags.

Beowulf lived on the far side of the Hydro in a row

of housing units that had gone badly downhill during the previous decade but that were being renovated by artistic people like Beowulf's parents. The artistic nature of Beowulf's parents accounted for his odd name. There were five other Arthurs in the Fourth Year Horizontal Band Module at the Level Eleven Education Center, and three Lancelots in his Vertical Grouping Unit alone. Thanks to the success of *The Dark Age Saga*, which had been running on Network Video for fifteen years, six nights a week with daily repeats at 1100 and 1500 hours for shift workers, an omnibus edition on Sundays and continuous showing of early episodes on Channel Seven, there were very few children under the age of fourteen who did not owe their names to the leading characters such as Merlin, Guinever, Gareth, Vivienne and Galahad. Arty knew personally only two: Beowulf Hopkins himself, whose name came from a cult serial on BBC3, and Jason Cropper, whose mom was simply old-fashioned.

Lance pushed the stridulating bell unit by the doorframe and from the Private Address module came Beowulf's mom's voice demanding, *"Now* who is it?"

"It's Lance and Arty Cooper, Mrs. Hopkins," Lance said, politely. In Mrs. Hopkins's view, he and Arty came from the wrong end of the walkway. Beowulf often remarked cryptically that if she knew what went on at their own end after dark, she might think twice before saying it. Beowulf himself tended to spend his leisure hours lurking around the shafts of the elevation modules, against the chance of an encounter with the Level Tenners. The Rose Street Gang were hoping devoutly for just one encounter with the Level Tenners before the Security Forces descended on them.

The interior of the Hopkinses' flat seemed to change shape every time Arty saw it. Mr. Hopkins was a great one for knocking down walls and erecting partitions. Like the Coopers he had cooking areas, eating areas, utility areas, which he referred to quaintly as rooms, and in the middle a huge empty space, with chairs, which he called the *living* room. Why not a dying room too? Arty wondered. When they went in Beowulf was squatting in the center of the living room in an attitude of irrascible dejection, stabbing angrily at a small control module with glowing LEDs.

"Hello, it's us," Lance said. "Where is it, then?"

Beowulf did not look up. "Where's what, then?" He banged the control module furiously against the side of his knee.

"The autogram."

"You tell me," Beowulf snapped. "In here, I suppose." He poked the module. "I can't get the bleeder out. I've only seen him once. He went on the blink as soon as he appeared."

"Let's have a look," Lance said, masterfully.

"It's malfunctioning. Looking at it won't help."

They wrangled over the module. Arty approached the Factcenter and dialed first Adscan, then Retail Leisure Aids, then Autograms. On the screen appeared a moving picture of an autogram, which was fairly pointless, Arty thought, as it looked, in the projection, just like an ordinary hologram or even a real person, masquerading as a hologram. This was followed by a list of available models. The autograms were heavily educational and featured Notable People from Living History, and one or two Ordinary People, who were not so educational, such as a Cave Man, a Roman Soldier, a Medieval Serf, a Seventeenth-Century Cavalier (get a Roundhead to match: big reduction!), an Eighteenth-Century Hussar with horse (horse extra and indispensable), a Nineteenth-Century Granny and a Twentieth-Century Commando. There history ended.

"Which one have you got?" Arty asked.

"Twentieth-Century Commando, I *suppose,*" Beowulf said. "He wasn't around long enough to find out." He pushed the discarded packaging toward Arty with his foot. "Captain Courage."

Arty stooped to pick up the box and at the same moment Lance contrived to press the correct combination of multifunctional keys. In the corner of the room, like a life-sized, out-of-focus reflection, the autogram was seen to materialize. Evidently it was still malfunctioning. It sidled about, one leg shorter than the other and with a curious dent in its hip as if someone had run into it with a right-angled object. It dipped and sashayed unpleasantly.

"What's it meant to do?" Arty asked, shying away as the image lurched too close.

"It's meant to talk for a start," Beowulf said, snatching back the control module from Lance. He pressed a key. The autogram began to utter in a low-pitched drawl that was entirely unintelligible.

"What's your name?" Arty asked it.

"It should only respond to my voice," Beowulf said. "It's personalized. What-is-your-name?" he said to the autogram, enunciating slowly as if speaking to an idiot.

The autogram turned its head. "Wha-a-a-at?" It developed a nervous tic in its cheek.

"Your name! Your handle—your monicker!" Beowulf shouted. He rattled the control module and the figure jolted into sudden and unattractive clarity.

There was a picture of Captain Courage on the box in Arty's hands. He was lean but muscular beneath his drab combat costume, and hefted a submachine gun in his capable hands. His teeth glinted in a dangerous white smile, his eyes were slitted, his jaw clenched askew with menace.

Arty looked from the picture to the real Captain Courage, or rather, to the illusion that purported to be Captain Courage. Captain Courage slitted his eyes, he smiled whitely; not only his jaw but his entire head was askew. He stooped purposefully, gripping the submachine gun. "Kitty-kitty-kitty," said Captain Courage. "Nice kitty. Come to Gran."

There was a considerable silence in the living room after this.

"What's it supposed to say?" Lance asked, finally. Beowulf grabbed the box from Arty and scowled at the data on the back.

"Drop your Kalashnikov or I'll blow you away," he complained.

"*Who's* a pretty boy, then?" said Captain Courage. His voice had become winsome and fluting. Beowulf lifted the control module and hurled it against the wall in disgust. Captain Courage contracted slightly and warped, as if seen through flawed glass. "Isn't it a nice day?" he said.

"That's Nineteenth-Century Granny," Arty said, light dawning. "They've programmed him with the wrong voice." It occurred to him that somewhere in the world there must be an autogram of Nineteenth-Century Granny snarling, "Drop your Kalashnikov or I'll blow you away."

"What's a Kalashnikov?" he asked.

"Get the whole set and be the envy of your friends!" said Adscan, which had been mumbling to itself in the Factcenter. "Imagine! A whole cohort of Roman Soldiers!"

"Imagine, a whole cohort of Nineteenth-Century Grannies!" Beowulf mimicked, savagely.

"Lovely weather for the time of year," Captain Courage observed, from his corner. He bobbed a horrid curtsey as Beowulf picked up the control module from beside his feet where it had rebounded from the plastic wall boarding. He fiddled with the keys and Captain Courage jived wildly, but did not go away.

"It's jammed," Beowulf said in alarm. "I can't switch him off."

"How are your cauliflowers coming along?" Captain Courage inquired.

"What's a cauliflower?" Arty said.

"Damn this for a lark," Beowulf said. "I'm going out. You don't catch me stuck here all day with Grandma Courage."

"What about us?" Lance demanded. "I told Mum we'd be out till dinner. It's her day at the Conversation Center.

She'll have put the security units on by now and we'll be locked out."

Arty seized his chance. "Let's go and play in the street," he said.

"I don't care where we play," Beowulf growled. He strode into the cooking area. His mother, who called it a kitchen, was stirring food in a pot over the stove. She went in for organic cookery. Captain Courage lurched after him.

"We're going out, Mum," Beowulf said. He put the control module on a shelf and began to tiptoe out of the kitchen.

"Get that thing out of here," Mrs. Hopkins said, "It gives me the creeps." Captain Courage leaned at a dangerous angle over the hot plate and writhed hideously in the steam.

"It's a very fine morning," said Captain Courage.

"He's stuck at 'on'," Beowulf said.

"I don't care where he's stuck as long as he's not stuck here," said Mrs. Hopkins. "I don't know; as soon as you get something you either lose it or break it."

"I'll leave it in the bedroom."

"No, you won't. You'll take it with you. I'm not having it hanging around here all day talking to itself."

"It only responds to my voice," Beowulf said.

"Take it *with* you."

The three of them trailed on to the walkway, and the door slammed shut behind them. After a moment Captain Courage followed them out, through the door.

"Are you going to whistle up the others?" Lance asked.

"What others?"

"Isn't it a nice day?"

"You shut up," Beowulf said, over his shoulder.

"The rest of the gang."

"I don't know that I want anyone to see me while *he's* around," Beowulf said, jerking his head toward Captain Courage, who jerked back, all over.

"Never mind the others," Arty said. "Let's go and play in the street."

"What's all this with the street?" Beowulf said.

"If you get me the wool, I'll knit one for you."

"*Will* you belt up?"

"He thinks because we're the Rose Street Gang we ought to go and play in Rose Street," Lance explained.

"It's three years since I've been in the street," Arty said. "I can't hardly remember what it looks like, even."

"Look," Beowulf said patiently to Arty, "we're the Rose Street Gang because we live in the Rose Street Development. We don't need to go out in the street."

"Where did I leave my umbrella?"

"The Level Tenners live in the Rose Street Development too," Arty said, "but everyone knows that they come from Level Ten. They've got identity."

"They've got a reputation."

"What a nice day," said Captain Courage.

"What price identity?" said Beowulf.

They were passing the Hydroponic Memorial Facility. With a practiced and unobtrusive flick of the wrist he spun the control module in among the sandbags. Captain Courage, after a moment's delay, staggered after it and began to float abstractedly between the palm trees murmuring, "Here, kitty. Kitty-kitty-kitty."

"Quick, before he notices," Beowulf said, and started to move away.

"Don't be daft," Lance said, "he doesn't know anything"; but he hastily joined Beowulf and Arty who were sauntering down the walkway looking innocent. They were scarcely level with Marks and Spencer before an enraged shout halted them.

"Oi! You lot! Come back here."

An irate Senior Citizen was advancing with unwonted nimbleness along the walkway, waving the control module above his head. Behind him came Captain Courage, emitting inarticulate squawks.

" 'Snot mine," Beowulf said, turning his back. " 'Snothing to do with us."

"I saw you!"

". . . Cauliauliflowowowers . . ."

"I saw you chuck it in," the Senior Citizen cried, and lobbed the control module toward them. "Take it away, Beowulf Hopkins, or I'll tell your dad."

"That's the trouble with this dump," Beowulf said, stooping to pick up the module. Captain Courage, who had disintegrated in flight, reassembled himself and glided in their direction. "Everybody knows everybody else."

"Lovely weather for the time of year."

"His feet don't touch the ground anymore," Arty said, as the Captain drifted abreast of them.

"Look," Lance said, "we're going to be out all day. Let's drop in at Tesco's and buy some fodder. Mum gave us a load of stuff, but we'll need more, and something to drink."

Tesco's was a hundred meters long and two meters deep. The boys roved from coin slot to coin slot, purchasing food and cans. As Lance fed in the coins Beowulf lifted the packages from the service apertures beneath. At the last one he took out a six-pack of Coolacola and slipped in the control module.

"Get moving," he said. They hurried on, leaving Captain Courage in animated conversation with a chewing gum dispenser.

"Well, fancy seeing you! Isn't it a nice day?"

"Are we going to collect the others or not?" Beowulf said as they continued down the walkway.

"Don't look around now," Lance said. "We're being followed."

They all looked around and stopped. A shopping area attendant was steaming up behind, followed by Captain Courage, now inclining several degrees from the perpendicular and chatting vivaciously with a rat that was running along the gap where the wall had subsided away from the ceiling.

"I saw you," the shopping area attendant said. "It's an offense, depositing foreign articles in the service apertures. It's an offense, that is. I could get you had up for that."

Wordlessly Beowulf received the control module and they resumed their journey.

"Let's go down to Level Ten at least," Arty said.

"There's a thought," said Lance. "Perhaps we could

leave him in the lift," but when they reached the elevation unit area a large and partially illuminated sign informed them: ELEVATION UNITS TEMPORARILY OUT OF ACTION. DANGER. MEN AT WORK.

There were no men at work.

"Can't we drop it down one of the shafts?" Lance said.

"We'll never get near," Beowulf said. "They'll have the deterrent beams switched on."

"If you get me the wool, I'll knit one for you."

"I don't suppose they'll be working either," Lance said, advancing hopefully toward the open shafts. "Ouch! They are, though."

"We'll have to use the stairs," Arty said. "We might meet the Level Tenners. Let's get the others, Lance. *Let's.*"

"If we can find a telecom that's not US," Lance said. "Where's the nearest?"

They walked on for another fifteen minutes toward the stairs and the telecom units that stood in a vandal-proof line against the wall. Most of them had been torn from their mountings.

"Got any money?" Beowulf asked.

"People like you ought to be locked up," Captain Courage rebuked him, severely.

"A fiver." Lance took out the coin and pressed it into the one slot that was not already plugged with super glue, super gum or Spicy Nibbles.

"Hello?" he said. "Hello!" he shouted, into the sticky mouthpiece. "Is that you, Kay?"

"You don't have to shout," said Kay Lambert, a block and a half away.

Lance said, "Look, Kay, we're going down a few levels"— Arty pricked up his ears —"and the lifts are US. We may need reinforcements. Interested?"

Kay's voice became thick and grainy at this point, but Lance understood him to say that he'd be there.

"Bring the others," Lance said. "We'll meet you at the head of the North Stairs. Half an hour? OK?" The line went dead. He replaced the oral module. "That should just give us time to get there," he said, "if we start walking now."

They started walking. Captain Courage followed, a few paces behind, veering and backing crazily upon his own axis.

"When we get to the next corner," Beowulf promised, "we'll lose him."

"My mum'd go spare if I lost something like that," Lance said. "They cost about three thousand each."

"Three thousand seven hundred and fifty, that one," Beowulf said. "My mum'll go spare too, but she'll be even sparer if I take this loony back again."

"Perhaps your dad can mend him," Arty said. "He's good with his hands."

"He'd need to be good with a hammer," Beowulf said, "to get anywhere with *him*."

"He's quite good fun, really," Arty said, wistfully. It was almost like having a mad but harmless adult in tow, and if they were going down to the lower levels an adult, even a mad and harmless one, could be nothing but an asset on those shadowy walkways below.

Beowulf shoved the control module into his hands.

"*You* look after him then, if you think so much of him. If anyone asks, he's yours." He stalked ahead, with Lance, and Arty trailed behind, experimentally depressing various keys. He felt that Beowulf simply did not understand Captain Courage. If you pressed *Volume Control* the Captain rose to shoulder height. *Forward Motion* made him reach for his gun and *Lateral Hold* made him fling himself defensively to the ground. In spite of curious looks from passersby, Arty kept his fingers on *Volume Control* and *Lateral Hold,* and the Captain swam alongside him, tossing off comments in response to Beowulf's distant remarks to Lance.

"Isn't it a nice day? If you get me the wool, I'll make one for you. How are your cauliflowers coming along?"

"What's a cauliflower?" Arty asked, but neither of the others answered.

"Where *did* I leave my umbrella?"

"What's an umbrella?" said Arty. "What's wool?"

They reached the head of the North Stairs just as Kay, with his sisters Guinever and Enid, approached from the opposite direction. Arty was glad to see them. Enid was a skinny little thing of small account, who rarely opened her mouth except to tell tales, but Guinever was the biggest of the lot, heavier than Lance, the eldest, and nearly as tall as Captain Courage had been when they first materialized him, although he was now almost a head shorter and correspondingly wider with an interesting cam amidships, as if someone had tried to twist him in half. When Arty saw the Lamberts loafing toward the stairwell he moved his finger to *Horizontal Hold*, which set the captain on his feet again, twenty or thirty centimeters above the floor, admittedly, but this was not obvious as he was in the rear, and it loaned him much-needed height. Guinever gaped.

"Who the hell is that?"

"Oh, it's just some old rubbish Arty picked up second-hand," Beowulf said.

"Kitty-kitty-kitty," said Captain Courage. He drew his gun. "Come to Gran."

"He won't be parted from it," Beowulf said, disgustedly.

"Don't take any notice," Arty whispered to Captain Courage.

Kay looked knowing. "It's one of those autograms, isn't it? From the History series."

"That's right," Arty said. "Twentieth-Century Commando."

"It looks more like a Twentieth-Century Drunk," Guinever said, as Captain Courage gyrated strangely in the background. "Anyway, what's the plan?"

"We're going to play in the street," said Lance.

"What!" said Arty. He jumped. Captain Courage jumped too, into the stairwell, where he hovered uneasily.

"You wanted to, didn't you? What d'you think, Beowulf? Now we've got this far . . ."

"Better than hanging around here with Grandma Courage," Beowulf said.

"Captain Courage is coming with us," Arty said, firmly.

"Captain Courage? *That?*" Guinever fell about, laughing.

"He's all right when you know how to handle him." Arty reeled in the Captain until he floated above the top step.

"Where *did* I leave my umbrella?" he said, plaintively.

"We've got plenty of food," Lance said.

"*We* stopped off and got some stuff at British Home Stores," Kay said. "I told Mum we were going down the levels so she won't be expecting us back till tonight. I can give her a buzz from Level One."

"Won't she mind?"

"Be too late to mind, won't it?" Guinever said.

"Do they have telecoms on Level One?" Arty said.

"We'll soon find out. Well, sooner or later . . ."

They started down. The staircases were short and the journey would have posed few problems, but when they reached Level Ten they discovered that the next descending flight was sealed off. DANGER! SUBSIDENCE! said a partially illuminated sign. In fact it said . . . ANGER! . . . UBSIDE . . .

"Ubside down," said Arty.

"What a nice day," said Captain Courage. "If you get me the wool . . ."

"Shut up!" they all cried together, except Arty. Arty had begun to notice that Captain Courage had abandoned Beowulf as a fellow conversationalist and had attached himself to Arty.

"Which way shall we go, then?" Beowulf asked. "The East Stairs are the nearest but they may be US too."

"Well, we might find a lift," Lance said, "and if we don't we'll just have to walk on to the South Stairs. I tell you what," he added, as they set off, "I reckon the planners that designed this place didn't want people going up and down between levels."

"Most people don't want to anyway," Kay said. "I mean, who'd want to be on Level Ten if they didn't have to?"

"But we *are* on Level Ten," Arty said, suddenly realizing it.

"Who's a pretty boy, then?"

"Look out for Level Tenners," Beowulf said.

The Level Tenners were a menacing myth rather than a dangerous reality. No one knew very much about them and what was unknown was invented, such as their numbers, reputedly around fifteen—or fifty. For a start they went to a different Education Center, on their own level (the Rose Street Gang were passing it now) and they came from the kind of families that the Coopers and Hopkinses and even the Lamberts would never associate with, even if the planners had encouraged upward mobility, or downward. Level Ten was a problem floor. Onto it were shelved all the tenants who could not or would not pay rent and who, as rumor had it, unscrewed their doors and used them as tables, chopped up their tables for firewood and kept the firewood in the bath. Level Ten dwellings were no more provided with grates and chimneys than were those on the other twelve levels, but the tenants constructed flues out of cans welded end to end and a sooty fog drifted along the walkways and landings at two meters above the floor.

Arty, now well behind, allowed Captain Courage to

dive in and out of it like the dolphins that he had seen on Network Video, frolicking in the sea. He had never seen the sea, although he thought that it might be nice to, one day. He had liked the look of it. He'd liked the look of the dolphins, too, although it seemed strange to think that anything so lithe and shiny could pack down into those preformed dehydrated steak fillets.

The walkways of Level Ten were sinisterly deserted. Accustomed to the relative bustle of their own level, the Rose Street Gang began to walk closer together and to look nervously over their shoulders. Lance even went back and collected Arty in an unprecedented access of brotherly concern.

"How far are we from the East Stairs?" Arty asked, as they hurried to catch up with the others. Captain Courage slithered in their wake, mumbling.

"About ten minutes, I should think," Lance said.

"We seem to have been walking for hours."

"Only one."

"That's just since we came down. It's hours since we left home. How soon can we eat?"

"When we get off Level Ten," Lance said. "Not long now."

"If the stairs are open."

"Well, if they're not we'll just have to go on to the next flight."

"But that'll be another hour!"

"We aren't stopping to eat on Level Ten," Lance said. Arty did not argue.

They were about a hundred meters from the head of

the East Stairs when Beowulf, who was a little in front, motioned them to halt and be quiet. They huddled together, even Guinever, listening, and Arty let Captain Courage throw himself on his front again. Up ahead they could hear voices, but the few overhead lights that were not broken were so obscured by smoke and accumulated grime that it was difficult for the gang to see even a dozen meters in front of them. However, after advancing pace by pace they began to make out a more solid thickening in the gloom, shadows less detailed but more substantial than Captain Courage. Arty took Captain Courage up forty centimeters until he was concealed in the murk, and held him there, praying that he would keep his mouth shut.

Kay whispered, "Level Tenners."

The others were silent except for Enid who began to whimper and clutched at Guinever.

"Gerroff," said Guinever, whose sense of sibling responsibility was about as highly developed as Lance's.

"Let's go back," Arty said. "Lance, let's go back. There's dozens of them."

"Trick of the light," said Lance.

"What light?" said Beowulf.

"We're not going back now," Guinever said, not even bothering to lower her voice. "We've always wanted to meet the Level Tenners, haven't we? Now's our chance."

"But we're not *ready*," Enid wailed. "They'll *massacre* us."

"*I'm* ready," Guinever said. She looked it. "I'm always ready."

One of the shadows at the stair head detached itself

from the mass and came toward them with threatening gait.

"Ooz'att'en?"

"You what?" Beowulf asked, almost politely.

"Ooz'att? Ooz'ere?"

"What?"

A derisive voice from the back of the group yelled, "They must come from upstairs. Foreigners! They don't even understand English!"

The first figure was now close enough for the Rose Street Gang to see that it was a youth, not very old but older than any of them, and bigger. He stopped, stared consideringly at them with his thumbs in his spiked belt and then called over his shoulder, "There's only six of them."

Seven, Arty thought. He was beginning to have an idea.

"There's twenty-two of us," the Level Tenner went on, to the gang. He sounded quite chatty. "By the time we've finished with you, you won't even match your own computer records."

The remainder of the Level Tenners began to issue like dark fumes from the stairwell. On they came. Even Lance and Guinever retreated slightly, and the others flattened themselves against the wall. Arty looked at the Level Tenners. They wore armor-plated trousers and rivet-studded tunics and steel-capped boots; one or two had horned helmets. All were armed with blunt instruments and sharp ones. They reminded Arty a little of Captain Courage, not as he actually was but as he had appeared on the package, only Captain Courage had had the lean fitness of a man who was trained for action and fed on red meat. The Level Tenners were lean with the scrawniness of those who trained for action on Spicy Nibbles and Coolacola. In spite of their numbers, Arty knew, they had certain disadvantages. They kept firewood in the bath, it was well known. They might have telecom and Network Video, if they didn't smash them up, but the chances of their ever having seen a hologram were remote. Certainly they would never have seen an autogram. Keeping back behind Enid and Kay he brought out the control module and scanned the keys as well as he could in the twilight.

"Put your hands up," said the leading Level Tenner.

They all raised both hands, except for Arty who put up one hand. The Level Tenner counted suspiciously as his merry men advanced to the attack.

"One of you only got one arm?" he demanded.

Another arm, apparently without anyone attached to it, reached down out of the smoke and aimed a submachine gun at the head of the Level Tenner. He stopped in midstride and stared at it, his mouth falling open. The arm was followed by a twisted smile and then by the whole of Captain Courage's twisted head. For once in his short life Captain Courage said the right thing. "People like you," he remarked, querulously, "ought to be locked up."

The Level Tenner stepped back. Captain Courage dived head-first out of the smoke and cavorted with langorous movements around the Level Tenner, flirting his machine gun skittishly, slithering wraith-like in and out of invisibility. Something nasty had happened to the Captain while he was up in the murk; bent, squashed, totally visible only from certain angles, he no longer resembled anything purely human, even to Arty, who knew what he was supposed to be. The Level Tenners had no such comforting knowledge. With cries of terror they turned and vanished into the darkling corridor pursued, for part of the way, by Captain Courage. "How are your cauliflowers coming along?" he asked them, but they were already too far away to hear.

The Rose Street Gang looked from Captain Courage to Arty and back to Captain Courage again.

"Aren't you glad he came with us?" Arty said.

They spent the night in a deserted hydroponic leisure facility on Level Five. Enid had brought along her pocket video and as they ate their rations they gathered around it to watch the latest episode of *The Dark Age Saga*. There were Vikings in it tonight, laying waste King Arthur's domain with fire and the sword, mainly the sword. It looked as if Sir Lancelot had been killed at the end, but they were sure that he couldn't really be dead, as he would be needed for tomorrow night. It was impossible to imagine *The Dark Age Saga* without Sir Lancelot.

"Perhaps he's been written out," Kay suggested, but no one believed him.

Later Arty dreamed that there were Vikings in the well of the North Stairs, woke sweating and was oddly reassured to see Captain Courage standing guard among the trees, glowing faintly. Without Arty's finger on the button he was inert, but every now and again he twitched violently, like a man suppressing hiccups.

In the morning they breakfasted and moved on down.

They met with no further obstacles; even some of the lifts were working, but between Levels Two and One they found three stairwells out of service and had to walk three-quarters of the way around the block, so it was well into the afternoon before they saw daylight seeping through the narrow exit that led to the street. They paused. It was a stirring moment, three years since Arty had been in the street and at least eighteen months since Lance had ventured so far. They stood in the strange cold light that came down to them from somewhere above the roof-tops.

The Rose Street Development stood massively among the crumbling and derelict remains of low-level housing, looking as if it had been not built but dropped among them from a great height and the impact had shaken their foundations. Behind them the building loomed, a cliff face, and a thin wind fumbled among the weedy rubble.

"What are all those little square holes?" Arty asked, pointing at one of the old houses.

"I dunno, winters or something," Lance said.

"Windows," Beowulf corrected him. "Dad's thinking of cutting one in our wall if he can get planning permission."

"King Arthur's got windows, Dumbo," Kay said. "Fancy not knowing what they are."

"His come to a point, though," Arty said.

"Well, here we are," Guinever said. "This is it. The street. What are we waiting for—let's play."

They moved off, Arty, as usual, in the rear with Captain Courage, who had begun to limp badly on the way down.

By daylight Captain Courage looked almost transparent, and he was sadly diminished. Even his voice was pale and weak. It seemed cruel and ungrateful to make him play and yet, inextricably attached as he was to his faulty control module, there could be no rest for him, no honorable retirement; better, surely, kinder and in a way more respectful, to put him out of his misery. When no one was looking, Arty maneuvered him across the roadway to the corner, where a sign saying Rose Street was affixed to the wall, and ground the control module under his heel.

"Good-bye," Arty said, and saluted, as best he knew how.

Captain Courage did not die instantly. He wavered and grew faint, rallied and glowed with a firm lambent light, and in that instant dwindled away among the weeds. "What a *nice* day," said a voice from the empty ether.

"Come *on*," Lance was shouting, from the next intersection. "It was you that wanted to play in the street," but Arty lingered on the corner, under the sign that hung swinging from one rusty bolt. He looked up at it and said, "I wonder, what's a rose?"

Urn Burial

ROBERT WESTALL

Ralph finished stowing his gear in his top-box: jar of Stockholm tar, bottle of cold tea, butties wrapped tight in his anorak to keep the tar smell out.

The sheepdogs were waiting, eager, keeping their eye in by herding the free-range hens around the farmyard and up the outside stair, from which they flew squawking in a cloud of feathers. Which sent the collies into their loll-tongued grins.

The scrambler started third kick; Ralph hated all machinery, but he had to use the scrambler. The trip up Fiend's Fell took too long on foot. He turned out of the farmyard, skidding in the pool of cow dung on the corner, and shot up onto the green-road.

The green-road zigzagged up the fell between black stone walls. Lined with last year's bracken, high and brown, with this year's bracken, so green you wanted to eat it, just curling through.

Ralph's heart lifted; good to be up and away on the
fell. But the turf of the green-road was slashed and rutted
by the other shepherds' scramblers, and the beat of his
own engine blatted back from the stone walls and that
spoilt it. Everything was getting spoilt these days. He
looked down at the village, tight huddle of gray houses
that had stood so right for so long. But spoilt by the shiny
metal barns and silos, the straggle of red-brick bungalows
leading nowhere. What did rich folk want in the country?

But great to climb up into the blue sky and quiet, with
the collies racing alongside, taking short cuts over the
walls to keep up.

A mile on, he parked, put on his anorak, sandwiches
in one pocket, tea and tar in the other. The top of Fiend's
Fell was too much even for scramblers. Steep as a roof,
tussocks of dead bleached grass bigger than a pop-star's
haircut, veined through with black burns deep as trenches
and treacherously overhung with tussocks. Hard enough
to keep your feet, sliding and panting. The only thing
that moved quick on the fell were the scatters of dirty
sheep fleeing upward before him. And the sheepdogs tiny
and black with white throats, flying up like birds, not attacking the sheep but instinctively cutting them into flocks,
moving them here and there, from habit. Sheepdogs were
like policemen, never off duty. But he whistled them to
heel; otherwise they'd run themselves too hot, then lie
in a burn to cool off and give themselves colic.

He kept to the wire fence, drawn like a pencil line
up the fell. The sheep grazed more heavily there; shepherds walked there; it avoided the burns; going was easier.

But depressing. Unlike stone walls, the fence gave the sheep no shelter in winter blizzards. The sheep drifted downwind till the fences stopped them, caught in the open, and there they died. There was always a scatter of skulls against the fence: sodden yellow fleeces like hearth-rugs with the bones delicately scattered on top, where the carrion crows had left them. Often, a smaller scatter lay tangled in, where a lamb had died with its mother.

It pained Ralph. The lowland sheep, fat white-faced Cheviots, were cosseted in barns for lambing, fed from hay bales in the bitter weather. The fell sheep, black-faced Herdwicks, were left all year round to live or die. Visited once a year, in July, to be counted and sheared, branded and dipped. He was getting ready for the shearing now. Counting the corpses, the survivors, number of well-grown lambs, twins. That, and his own particular brand of mercy, the Stockholm tar.

The sheep got whicked, see? Cut themselves on the wire, or leaping wildly over the stone walls in one of their sudden, inexplicable panics. Then the blow-flies laid their eggs in the open wounds, and the foul white grubs hatched out and ate the sheep alive.

He spotted their first victim, running well behind its group with a humping rocking-horse gait, the raw red patch on its rump clearly visible in the sunlight. He sent off the dogs, Jet to the left, Nance right, cutting their wide circles across the tussocks, coming in behind, penning the whole group into an angle where the fence met an old black wall.

"Coom by, Jet! Coom by, Nance!" But he was just

making noises. The dogs, veterans, knew what he wanted better than he did himself.

Soon, stillness. The sheep huddled together, staring at him hostile with their strange yellow oblong eyes. The dogs lay staring at the sheep, tongues lolling, edging forward on their bellies inch by inch. Keeping the sheep just scared enough to be still, not scared enough to try a wild leap over the wall.

"Lay doon, Jet!" He waded among the dense-packed wooly bodies that shifted uneasily; felt their sharp feet through the leather of his boots; grabbed the victim, clenching it backward between his knees, and reached out the tar. It glugged, black and oily, onto the red bleeding wound big as a man's hand. And soon the evil maggots swam upward, drowning as they died.

The victim would live; the grubs hadn't reached a vital part, the spine or bowel. It glared up at him with eyes that comprehended nothing except terror. He let it go, checked the others and called off the dogs. The little flock went off like a rocket.

"I am the good shepherd," he thought sadly. "I know my sheep and am known of them." He never heard that reading, sitting beside Mam in chapel, without smiling. Sheep must have been brighter in Jesus' time. To these sheep, he was just one more terrifying monster in their terror-stricken lives. Why? Cows came to him, pigs were friendly, even the lowland Cheviots. He knew so little of these sheeps' lives. Fifty-one weeks in the year they were up here alone in the wind and snow and rain. What went on, to make them so *frightened*?

The top of Fiend's Fell was a lonely place. Always had been. Take away the man-made fence, it might be a hundred years ago, ten thousand . . . if he himself fell into the black gulley of an overhung burn, broke his neck, would they ever find his body? Or would his bones lie, picked white as the sheep's, till they rotted away?

He glanced around, suddenly uneasy. He had dipped down into a bowl of the land. All around him stretched the brown swell of the fell. Apart from fences, not a work of man in sight. He shuddered, despite the July sun.

Don't be daft; the dogs would bring help; *they'd* find him. He called them, looked into their warm brown eyes, played with their floppy velvet ears. At least he knew his sheepdogs and was known of them.

Get on; nearly lunchtime.

He ate it sitting against the cairn that marked the top of the fell. The dogs, as usual, coaxed half his sandwiches out of him. Spam, cheese, pickle, they loved them all. Nosed the greaseproof paper carefully, to make sure of the last crumb. Then went off hunting something live for the rest of their dinner. Never still, sheepdogs. He could see their black feathery tails wavering out of some shallow burn. They moved toward each other from opposite ends, hoping to trap something tasty and stupid between them.

Over-full, he drowsed, surveying the sunlit fell through half-closed eyes. Why *Fiend's* Fell? Folk hereabouts didn't call it that; just "t'fell." But the Ordnance Survey map at school named it quite clearly. When he asked, people just shrugged and said it was some daft idea of people in London, who had nowt better to do.

He felt the change come. A gentle pressure against his left cheek that wasn't wind, but a new faint warm dampness. He just knew, even though the sky was still blue, that it'd be raining by four. Heavy, maybe thunder.

No fun on the open fell in a thunderstorm. Last time, the only dry spot on him had been two inches under his belt. He'd dripped a pool in Mam's kitchen four foot wide. No shelter ont' fell, see? None at all.

Suddenly urgent, he got up to get on. It was then he noticed some stones had fallen off the other side of the cairn and were lying on the heather.

Nobody knew who made the cairns. They'd always been there. Six-foot pyramids of stones big as your head. Maybe the old drystone-wallers put them there. Maybe they were older than the wallers. Some said that in the dim and distant past every shepherd starting out from the valley brought a stone, and the cairns were built that way. Certainly there were no loose stones handy for miles. The one certainty was that if you were a hill-shepherd, you didn't let the cairns fall down. After a blizzard, they were the only familiar thing in a totally changed landscape. They looked after cairns, did shepherds. He picked up the first fallen stone, and leaned over to put it back.

Funny! There was a piece of metal sticking out, like the tip of a bricklayer's trowel set upright. Corroded into white spots, like aluminum. He pulled at it, but it stuck fast. And it was too slim and whippy for a bricklayer's trowel. Intrigued, he pulled out two more stones. But the thing wouldn't budge. He could tell from the way it grated against the stones that there was a lot more of it down inside. He pulled out more stones, laying them down careful and handy. Wouldn't take long to rebuild. . . .

Ten minutes revealed two feet more of the metal; a pointed blade with a thin tapering shaft below. A spear? No, the old knights used iron, which would've rusted. And he remembered from school the Romans used bronze. And it was definitely fixed to something deep inside. He looked in distress at the topless cairn, stones strewn in all directions. Looked at his watch; his lunch hour was over. And rain coming. But he *had* to know. Oh well, he could work overtime, get wet. . . .

After another half an hour, four foot of spear was showing. Except it definitely wasn't a spear. Too whippy, modern. More like the radio aerial on a tank. Not a metal he knew. Too yellow for aluminum, too white for brass. And the lower shaft, protected from weather by the cairn, glistened strangely.

The dogs, aware their usual routine had been broken, had come back and were lying watching, heads cocked on one side. He felt guilty about his boss, about the cairn.

But he had to know. Maybe it was something for the Ministry of Defense, like the big towers over Middleton-in-Teesdale way? But then, why *hide* it? Maybe it was the Russians. . . . He attacked the cairn with renewed vigor, appalled at his own powers of destruction.

Finally his hand, delving around another stone, touched something smooth and cool and rounded. He pulled away the stone, saw something like a bit of car windshield. Darkness inside, and something inside the darkness. Now he was throwing away stones any old how, making the dogs back away. He cleared a foot of windscreen. Something metal and complicated inside. Lying on a fur rug? He cleared more stones. More metallic thing, more fur rug. A glass dome? Well, more like Perspex; more shaped like a cigar. *Was* it the Russians? His belly crept.

He snatched one more stone away, and the whole side of the cairn collapsed.

Then he realized it wasn't just a fur rug in there. Underneath was the shape of a leg, a shoulder. Still half hidden, a bump that could be a head. Quite still, under the glass.

A coffin.

He leapt back. Staring at the wild, spreading destruction of the cairn, he knew he'd done a dreadful thing. Stared around, expecting punishment. But no punishment came, and he felt terribly alone. He looked at the dogs, but they just looked back, puzzled why he didn't go back to work. He felt even more alone. Then he decided, if he put all the stones back very carefully, under the indifferent blue sky, no one would ever know.

That was best.

But when he went back (careful not to look at the man under the striped fur rug) he noticed the coffin was in two halves; a top and a bottom hinged together. And there were three things a bit like the locks on a suitcase; except funny-shaped and far too thin, of the same yellowish metal. He thought he could see how they worked. . . .

One peep? Surely that wouldn't do any harm? He wrestled with himself; began to replace the stones.

Then undid the locks with a rush, one, two, three. They

snapped back, making the coffin resound like a drum. He raised the lid a fraction.

No smell of foulness, like what lingered inside the sheep's skulls along the fence. A gentle clean smell, like the ointment Mam used to put on his knee when he grazed it. A *safe* smell. It gave him the courage to tip the lid back.

The snarling behind brought him out in a cold sweat.

But it was only the dogs, backing away, bellies pressed to the ground, ears flat to their skulls and the skin of their lips puckered up, revealing long teeth brown at the roots. The hair on their backs stood up in arched ridges, and their tails were bushed up, enormous. And always they retreated farther, farther. . . .

Oh, they'd get over it. . . .

He turned back to the coffin, reassured by the antiseptic smell. Who was it, wrapped in the fur rug? If he pulled it back a little . . .

But when he touched it, he realized it wasn't a man in a fur rug. It was only an animal buried there. He laughed to himself; he'd seen plenty of dead animals. But what animal? Six foot long, curled up on its side. A big cat like a tiger, only the stripes were fainter, narrower, brown. Too slim . . . a cheetah? . . . that kind of frailty, gentleness. No, too big for a cheetah. And the front paws were long and delicate, like human hands. And the hind legs made up half the length of the body.

He got in close, peered at the dead face. The closed eyes had been huge, but the closed mouth quite small, less frightening than a dog's. He touched the shoulder.

The fur was soft, dense, fine; the muscles solid and supple, but intensely cold. Then he saw the belt it was wearing, woven from the yellow metal. And the triangular insignia hung around its neck. And he somehow knew it had walked upright like a man. Thought like a man. Had never walked this earth.

Well, not *born* here. He straightened, looked up at the blue sky. The blue sky looked back, indifferent. Were they up there somewhere, hidden behind the sun? Watching? Would they come? Punish? He *had* done a dreadful thing. He just stood and shook and watched his dogs, tiny black dots now, turn on their heels and vanish over the rim of the fell, heading for home.

The dogs knew he had done a dreadful thing.

He might have stood there and shaken forever, if his eye hadn't lit on the top of the spear, still protruding from the coffin. He saw it with great clarity against the blue sky; the marks of corrosion on it. It had stood there a long, long time. The grave was old, old. As old as the cairn, on which Granda had sat, as a boy. Whoever They'd been, They were gone, gone, light-years across space.

He relaxed; his sin was his own. He could undo it, if he put back the cairn, and no one would ever know. But before he did . . . he suddenly wanted to know what the creature had looked like in life. He lay on his side beside the coffin. The edges of the stones cut into his hip, as he raised both hands to the creature's face, so close to his own. His arms trembled but he pushed up the eyelids, cold and supple as the rest.

The creature stared at him; cat's eyes, thin slits. There

was a sense of hunching-up in the face, shock, pain. Same look as he'd seen on the face of a mummified Egyptian cat, on the school trip to the British Museum. He wondered, if he turned the body over, whether he'd find some terrible wound . . . but that was unthinkable. He let the eyelids drop shut, smoothed their fur where his fingers had ruffled it. Marveled at the tiny whirling patterns of hairs on the long slim nose. Stroked the head gently, the thin ears through which the sun shone, outlining veins frozen forever. Just like stroking a pet cat.

He sat up. A wound? Was this a warrior, a casualty from some star-battle, brought for burial to innocent bystanding Earth? A warrior buried with his weapons? For the coffin was full of objects, packed as closely around the creature as sardines in a can. He reached for the smallest object, a red-luster capsule like a duck egg. Fiddled with the strange catch, sideways, up. And the egg broke open, the top half sliding around the bottom, smoothly.

Inside, a pale green substance, a few tiny bubbles caught frozen on its surface. He sniffed cautiously; it smelt good, somewhere between cheese and peppermint. He poked the surface, leaving a fingerprint like in butter. Sucked his finger.

Wham! He shot upright. Felt so *good*! His lungs breathed deeper, sucking in air of their own accord. His heart beat faster, bigger, like a strong animal inside his ribs. A curling pleasure and warmth ran right down into his toes. His eyes . . . it was like looking through the very best kind of binoculars. Beetles seemed to be crawling on every blade of grass; he'd never seen so many beetles. The distant fence, he could follow every kink in its wire, even though it was half a mile away. And his ears! The world was a symphony of rushings and hissings and clickings and sighings, and he knew what every click and hiss was, and everything was in its place.

He thought, "I am God." Then corrected himself. "I know how God feels." Like on Christmas morning, he plunged for the next egg. A lustrous black this time, full of blue paste. Pressed in his finger and raised it to his lips . . .

His lips froze. No feeling. Couldn't move them. Tried to speak, shout. All that came out was a splutter of breath. The deadness crawled back across his tongue, down his throat. . . .

He forgot how to breathe. Pulled his lips apart with his fingers; drove the bottom of his dying lungs to suck in breath, while his whole face went numb and his eyes gave out and the world went black.

He came to, lying in the heather, still trying to breathe with the shallow bottoms of his lungs. But slowly the cold receded, till he could feel his fingers on his chin when he pinched it and finally he could hear himself saying, over and over again, "Oh dear, oh dear, oh dear!"

He put the black egg back, ignored the other four. Lifted out the longest object—dull blue-black metal. A weapon? He turned it over and over, holding it by its various projections till it felt right. One end fitted naturally and softly onto his shoulder, and a lens came up to meet his eye. (Though he had to stretch; the creature had a longer neck.)

The front edge of the handle in his right hand seemed to move a little . . . a trigger? But suppose he was holding the weapon back to front? Might blow his shoulder off. . . .

He might never have fired it. He disliked killing anything. Always took a day off work when they sent the sheep to market, so he didn't have to see them go. The boss teased him, but turned a blind eye. No, he never would've fired, except that five black crows flew silently across the telescopic lens. He hated crows; they picked the eyes out of new-born lambs.

He squeezed the trigger.

It didn't kick like a shotgun. But there was a bang that deafened him, even far off. When he opened his eyes, not only had the crows vanished, but a huge gouge, like a trench, had been sliced out of the hillside. Bemused, he ran across. It was clean-edged, as if sliced with a knife. No explosion, no burning. As he looked, a worm came wriggling out of the sliced banking and fell to the bottom of the trench. Well, half a worm. But it still had its saddle intact; it would live. Another worm fell out, and another. Like the time he'd helped the gravedigger. He kept staring at the wound in the earth. It looked so official, like it had been dug by council workmen.

He walked back to the cairn, careful to keep his hand off the trigger. He didn't want his foot suddenly, surgically vanishing. At the cairn he turned and stared at the gash, still not quite able to believe *he*'d done it. He raised the weapon, aimed at the gash and fired again. Another earth-shattering bang. But when he opened his eyes this time, the gouge had totally vanished. Everything was as it had been. Five black crows, miraculously restored, flapped their way out of the circle of the telescopic sight.

Again he ran across, wondering if he was going crazy. Not a sign of damage anywhere, not even a scorch mark. Though there must be some very muddled worms underground. . . .

He made the gulley three more times; cancelled it three more times. Those worms mustn't know whether they were coming or going. He laughed, then stopped abruptly, not liking the sound of his own laughter in that silent bowl of the fell. Finally, feeling a bit sick and with a headache starting, he put the weapon back in its proper place.

It was then he noticed the helmets. Two, side by side, above the creature's head. One was matt black, seemed to repel the light and lurk in its own shadow. It was dented, the visor scorched. A war-helmet . . . He pulled his hand back; sick of weapons.

The other, though, had to be peaceful. It glittered with patterns, red and blue and gold, arranged in playful shapes that seemed to move under his eyes. A fun-helmet. He picked it up, put it on. It was far too big for him, probably to accommodate the creature's huge ears. But as he pulled the glittering visor down over his eyes, he felt little thin gentle things, like cat's whiskers, reach out from the inside wall of the helmet and touch his eyes, ears, start growing up his nostrils, and into his mouth. He cried out and tried to snatch the helmet off.

Too late; he was already in a different place.

Darkness. Then a door swung up, and a ladder swung out beneath his feet. And he was staring at hundreds of the creatures: black or gray, striped or spotted. They stared up at him, upright, still and silent. So he should have been afraid. Except their eyes were the warm blinking eyes of a cat by the fire, and the air was filled with a profound soft purring.

He stepped out onto the steps. Immediately, every right paw was raised in silent salute; long furry fingers with claws retracted; black pads on the palm. He saw the shadow of his own right arm shoot up in response, around the edge of his helmet; and there was striped fur on it.

They opened their mouths and whispered:

"Prepoc! Prepoc! Prepoc!" They breathed it with wonder, and he knew it was his name. Then he walked down the yellow metal steps, soundlessly, as if he was walking on fur. He was among them and they were pressing in, rubbing softly against every part of him. And there was no aloneness anymore, no cold, no fear, no hunger. *Prepoc! Prepoc! Prepoc!*

At last it ended, and they were gone, their purring fading on the wind. Only a lone creature remained, and he knew with a stir in his body that she was female and he knew her. Then there were three more, striped, female, nearly grown and all exactly alike. Then four more males, scarcely half grown and all exactly alike. And then they all ran together, under an orange sky with twin suns, under great craggy cliffs and hills, across tumbled fields of giant boulders, warm under his feet from the light of the twin suns. And it was a delight for stiff and cramped muscles to leap and climb, to fall and twist and land surefooted without pain.

▲ ▲ ▲

Eventually, the joy ended.

Dusk; and all around him yellow fighting-ships were climbing into the sky on thunderous flame. Hovering.

Waiting for him. And again the great assembly of creatures pressed in around him. Only there was no purring, but sadness, great sadness now. And he climbed the metal steps, and they raised their black paws, and the steps were drawn in and the door shut and there was darkness.

Then the helmet retracted its little whiskers from his ears and eyes, from up inside his nostrils and from out of his mouth. And he reached up and raised the visor, and he was sitting on the fell and the clouds were massing heavy and on his hand he felt the first spot of rain.

He pulled off the helmet. A memory-helmet; a bit like the family photographs that every soldier carried around in his wallet. . . .

But he was glad. I'm glad you made it home, Prepoc, warrior, hero, leader.

Then he saw Prepoc lying on the open fellside, with the first drops of earth-rain marking dark patches on his fur.

He put the helmet back, and got the coffin lid closed quickly. The rain came down in torrents, soaking him, making his hands slip on the stones as he carefully rebuilt the cairn, which glistened dully in the green rainlight.

Then he raised his right arm in the same salute, and turned wearily for home. The dogs were waiting, as he crossed the crest and home came in sight, far down the valley. The dogs were soaked, miserable, slinking tail-down through the downpour. But Ralph walked feeling like a god. Nobody else on earth would ever know what he knew. Prepoc, hero. Prepoc my friend, dead among the stars yet here on earth to touch.

He'd never tell a soul. . . .

Then suddenly he thought of Mam, endlessly slaving to make ends meet on a widow's pension. Cleaning for women who were rude, and she didn't dare answer back or they'd sack her. Mam, fallen asleep in her chair at the end of the day, mouth open and snoring, ugly with weariness.

Prepoc had so much, and Mam so little. Suppose, next time he came, he took Prepoc's red egg with the stuff that made you feel great. . . . It would make Mam feel great. Or he could sell it for money . . . to ICI, maybe. They could find out what it was made of, and make it for themselves. It would make their fortunes. . . . Mam wouldn't have to slave anymore.

But they'd ask him where he got it. Keep on at him till he told them. He knew he wasn't clever enough to lie. Then they'd come and dig up Prepoc, and cut him up in little pieces to find out all about him. Or stuff him and put him in some museum to be gawped at.

Oh, Prepoc!

Oh, Mam!

He stopped, stared back at the cairn, just visible over the swell of the fell. He hovered piteously, torn in half, so the dogs turned back, paws upraised, and stared at him impatiently.

Oh, Mam! Oh, Prepoc!

There was a flash from the cairn; a white flare in the storm-sky. The same bang the weapon had made. . . .

Then the cairn was no longer there.

Oh, Prepoc, friend, did you *know* I was going to betray you?

No. It must have been some delayed-action auto-destruct, triggered off inevitably once the grave had been opened and the discovering human had retired to a safe distance. The thought was a kind of comfort. . . .

But now, he had *nothing*. Nothing to remember Prepoc by. Nothing to prove it hadn't been a dream, as the years went by, and the memory faded. He felt bitter, cheated. It was *worse* than never finding anything.

Oh, Prepoc, did you *have* to?

He pulled up the zipper on his anorak higher, against the rain. It was then that he found it. A small curl of striped wet fur, caught in the anorak zipper handle.

With trembling fingers he freed it, and got out his water-proof cigarette case and put it inside. It nestled wetly against the three Woodbines.

Thank you, Prepoc. Feeling a lot better, he trudged down the hill to the bike.

In a Ship Called Darkness 3

CHRISTOPHER LEACH

ONE

His best uniform stiff and sharp against his throat and wrists, the old scars aching, the gold eagle shining at his breast, the 2nd Jupiter Campaign ribbon latched above the wings, he waited in the silent outer office and swung his corded cap in his fingers. He was a tall, thin man with a hard brown face and cropped gray hair, older than he looked. He had waited for this call a long time, and now that it had come he was one-hundred-per-cent ready. Or so he thought.

A light woke in the recognition-panel to the left of the door.

"You may go in now, Captain Stern," said the clipped, inhuman voice, neither male nor female.

He stood up and his body complained, wanting rest. He forced it forward and the door closed behind him.

The Marshall sat behind his oval desk, flanked by two

senior officers. Framed by the great window the silent city showed its towers and bright man-made trees.

Stern saluted.

"Sit down, Captain," said the Marshall.

Stern took off his cap and lowered himself into the hard chair.

There was a silence. The Marshall's desk was empty of papers, documents. No reports. One of the senior officers was smiling slightly. The Marshall, a younger man than Stern, bright-eyed, without war experience, scarless, graduate of the Youth Academy, a former Student of the Year, linked well-tended fingers.

"Sorry to have kept you waiting, Captain."

Stern said nothing.

"How are you now?" said the Marshall.

"Very fit," said Stern.

"Ready to resume duty?"

"You know I am."

"You grunted as you sat down," said one of the officers. Stern looked at him: They were all so young, these days.

"Habit," he said.

"Of course," said the Marshall. He leaned back in his chair. "Cigarette, drink?"

"It's been over a year," said Stern.

"You'd rather we get to the point, yes?" said the Marshall. "I understand. *We* understand." The officers nodded. "Why do you think you're here, Captain?"

"Promotion," said Stern. "A new command."

There was another silence. The officer to the right of the Marshall had stopped smiling. In this soundproofed room Stern could hear the quick shuttle of his own breath.

"Correct," said the Marshall. He opened a drawer in his desk and brought out an insignia and placed it on the highly-polished surface. Light caught the fake diamond and it blazed. "Congratulations, *Major*."

Stern relaxed.

"Thank you, Marshall," he said. He reached forward, but the Marshall covered the rainbow-glitter with his hand. Stern stayed reaching, then sat back. The old fear returned.

"It's conditional," said the Marshall.

Stern's breath came faster and he swallowed behind closed lips. He put one hand over another on his thigh, hoping he looked composed, military, unaffected.

"I'm not returning to the Fleet," he said, and it was not a question.

"No," said the Marshall.

"I don't want a desk job," said Stern. Anger warmed him and he stretched his neck in the close-fitting collar. "I haven't waited a year to . . ."

"Calm yourself, Major," said one of the officers. "Listen to the Marshall."

"You have promotion and a new command," said the Marshall. "A new duty, a new responsibility." He paused. "We want you to take over Darkness 3."

All Stern's dreams collapsed.

"You're joking," he said.

TWO

The taxi stopped and the door slid back. Stern got out, the door closed, and the driverless bubble sped away

to another call. He went into his house. Both his sons
were now at the Academy: He would never get used to
the lack of greeting, the quiet. He put his cap on the
hall table and went into the kitchen. There was a smell
of cooking, and he found he was very hungry. His wife
turned from the steaks. Her face smoothed itself as she
saw the insignia pinned below the eagle. She kissed him.

"At last!" she said. "Congratulations!"

"Yes," he said.

"The boys will be pleased," she said. "They've taken
a lot of teasing."

"Yes," he said. He took a bottle of wine from the cabinet and filled a glass. He unbuttoned his collar and sat
down facing the window and the bowl of Venutian roses.
"There's a condition," he said.

"Well, we expected that . . ." she said.

"They want me to take over Darkness 3," he said.

"They *what*?"

He drank some of the wine: the last of the raid on
the King's cellars, on Jupiter, long ago. "Cheers," he said.

"You're joking," she said.

"That's what *I* said."

"It's a convict ship," she said. "A Dispatcher."

"Tell me something I don't know."

"But you're part of the Fleet!"

"Not anymore."

"But Majors don't fly Dispatchers."

"They do now." He looked up at her concerned face
and wondered again how much he could safely tell her.
She was his second wife: His first, the mother of his two
sons, had died in a demonstration. Anne was new, and

young, and . . . trusting. "They say they have Morgan," he said softly, and watched carefully for her reaction.

Her face stayed concerned: for him, not for Morgan.

"I've heard nothing on the Screen," she said.

"They're keeping it a secret until he's gone," said Stern. "They want me to dispatch him."

The hotplate cut out: The steaks were ready. She turned back to attend them.

"Why you?" she said.

"I frankly don't know," he said, although he suspected. He drank some more wine. "I'm starving."

"Ready now," she said, and took the warm plates from the rack. "Perhaps it's a test. Perhaps they're testing you."

He finished the wine and held the empty glass in his hands.

"I think it's . . . more than that," he said, and regretted the words.

"What, for instance?" she said.

He laughed, covering up.

"If I can fly a Dispatcher, I can fly anything," he said. "A trial run: Perhaps that's the test."

"Then you've agreed to do it?" she said.

He tapped the insignia with one finger.

"Looks like it," he said.

"When do you have to go?" she said.

He looked out of the window at the pale green, cloudless sky.

"Tomorrow," he said. "Early."

THREE

There were three ships called Darkness. *Darkness One* served the penal settlement of the planet Samson; *Two,* the planet Absalom; and *Three,* the planet Cain, where the most depraved were sent: those who had plotted against the State. Each ship was fitted with a Dispatcher, through which murderers and ringleaders and the insane were flung into space.

At the Complex, thirty miles outside the city, at seven the next morning, Stern met his crew. They were a shabby lot: stained, unpressed uniforms; slack in coming to salute; the co-pilot yawning, showing teeth that needed attention. Yet Stern sensed in these undisciplined men an undercurrent of excitement, perhaps even fear. They were edgy and restless, they laughed too much; they were reluctant to face him directly, their eyes shifting elsewhere; and again the nervous laughter. His spine grew cold.

The ship itself reflected the crew's indolence. A once-proud Bulwark 7, it was out of fashion now, superseded, its insides gutted, cages in place of those marvelous battlescreens and precision weapons; the addition of a Dispatcher at its rear, robbing the craft of a once-beautiful, sleek, uninterrupted line. Gone too were the silver and gold: The ship was now a dull black, already showing the marks of travel and the rage of its prisoners.

"Name?" said Stern.

"Lomas," said the co-pilot.

"Lomas, *sir,*" said Stern; "or *Major.*"

The Lieutenant showed his bad teeth.

"Come down in the world, isn't it, Major," he said, "taking out a Darkness?"

"I don't like familiarity," said Stern. "Is . . . Are the prisoners aboard?"

"Due any moment, sir," said Lomas.

Stern drew him to one side.

"Something wrong with your men?"

"In what way, Major?"

"They seem . . . uncertain. Slack."

"They suspect something's up," said Lomas. "We've never had a Major before. Working with the dregs tends to make you . . . apprehensive. You begin to think . . ."

"Do they know about Morgan?" said Stern, softly.

"Morgan? No. *I* only heard an hour ago. They . . ."

"Prisoners coming now, sir!" called one of his men.

Perched on the high monorail the prison train looked frail and insubstantial, but the faces behind the unbreakable circular windows did not: pressed forward, their punishment-collars glowing that strange acid yellow, they were a gallery of hatred. The windows of the last box were shuttered, and Stern could not take his eyes from those gray, metallic strips.

The Lieutenant unclipped the punishment-master from his belt, keeping the thumb of his right hand an inch above the button.

"Let them come!" he shouted.

The doors of the first box opened and the prisoners stepped out onto the narrow silver platform. Some were weak and had to be supported by the stronger. They began to move down the ramp to the ship. One, a big man with a crown of thick red hair, saw Stern.

"We're privileged, brothers," he said. "We have a Major to take us home."

"Home?" said an older, graying man.

"Keep moving," said Lomas.

One by one the boxes emptied. And still the shutters of the last had not lifted. The platform was deserted now.

"OK!" shouted Lomas. "Get him out!"

One of the crew banged on the far door. It opened and an armed guard came into view. He motioned to someone inside. Stern leaned forward.

The prisoner was small and dark. On his black prison clothes he wore the red circle of the most dangerous.

"That's Morgan?" said Lomas.

"They say it is," said Stern. "There was never any photograph. His men never betrayed him, gave a description."

"Someone's betrayed him now," said Lomas.

They watched the two guards bring the most wanted man in the country, the legendary resistance-leader, the supreme revolutionary, down the ramp to the ship.

"He's smaller than I thought," said Lomas.

"Size doesn't come into it," said Stern.

"Still, he's disappointing," said the Lieutenant.

"OK, boys—take him inside."

As Morgan passed them he looked first at Lomas, and then at Stern. He had a face like a captured animal: alert, never still, seeking escape.

"Good morning, gentlemen," he said.

Lomas did not respond, but Stern nodded.

Inside the ship the chanting began. Lomas sighed.

"Time for the happy pills," he said.

FOUR

Every prisoner eagerly accepted a pill, and soon there was a blissful silence as, slumped in their cages, they lived their separate fantasies. Only Morgan, alone in the restraint-chamber near the Dispatcher, had refused that sweet oblivion, and, strapped to the wall, rested his head against the pulsing metal and closed his eyes as the engine roared and the ship surged from the Earth.

To Stern it was like being reborn. He had not flown a ship for over a year, but the old expertise came as naturally as breath. He loved the power under his hands, the problems of the world falling back; the ship threading its way through the satellite-forests, and out into clear, star-hung space.

Once they were past the fiery orb that was the sun Orgo, they could relax: the ship on automatic, and coffee and sandwiches served.

Lomas was studying his instructions.

"Thirty for the Dispatcher," he said. "Seventy-three for Cain. Nothing here about Morgan."

"I know about Morgan," said Stern. "I'll deal with him."

Lomas glanced at the Major's face, half-illumined by the green glow of the computer panel.

"Care to tell me?" he said. "Sir?"

"You know better than that," said Stern. "Just leave things to me."

"Yes, sir," said Lomas, and smiled.

When Stern had finished his coffee, he tossed the carton

into the disposer, brushed crumbs from his lap, and stood up.

"I'm going to take a look around," he said.

"Want one of my men to come with you?" said Lomas.

"No," said the Major. "I know my way around a Bulwark."

"Yes, sir," said Lomas. Alone now, he switched on the Screen and settled down to watch how Earth was doing in the Alpha Football Cup.

Stern walked through the black corridors of the quietly humming ship. In each cage the prisoners still stayed slumped against each other, eyes open, stupid smiles fixed on their dreaming faces. Stern moved on, swiftly.

The two guards outside the restraint-chamber came to attention.

"Relax," said Stern. "No trouble?"

"No, sir," said the taller, a sergeant. "He's not made a move."

"Go get yourselves some coffee," said Stern.

They looked at each other.

"We're not allowed to leave here," said the sergeant. "Strict orders."

"What can he do?" said Stern.

They were silent.

"You know who he is?" said Stern.

Once again they looked at each other.

"No," said the smaller. "But we can guess."

"Give me your P-master," said Stern to the sergeant. "Now go and get some coffee." They made to protest. "And that's an order. I take full responsibility."

"*One* of us will go, sir," said the sergeant.

"Very well," said Stern. "Now open up." He went into the restraint-chamber. It smelled like a zoo. "Close the door."

The sergeant hesitated; and closed it.

FIVE

Morgan sweated in his thick straps. The tip of his tongue touched the center of his top lip, and was slowly withdrawn.

"Thirsty?" said Stern.

"I have something," said Morgan, and moved his body to show a can of beer. He squirmed in the creaking leather. "You can get me out of these."

"I can't do that," said Stern. He sat down on the warm, gently vibrating floor, drew up his legs and rested his wrists on his knees, his right hand loosely grasping the P-master. "So you're Morgan," he said.

"No," said the man. "No, I am not."

"You're *not* Morgan?" said Stern, and the fear came back. He gave a soft laugh that sounded strange. *"They've got the wrong man.* They all say that."

The man drank some beer and held the can in hands that did not tremble.

"Who are you, if you're not Morgan?" said Stern.

The man looked away.

"Does it matter?" he said. "I'm for Dispatching." He looked back at Stern. "You the ranking officer?"

"Yes."

The man inched forward until the straps straightened, and held.

"Let me off at Cain," he said, quietly.

"I can't do that. Orders."

The man nodded.

"Go away," he said.

"If you're not Morgan, who are you?" said Stern again.

"My name is Patrick. Evan Patrick. I'm a printer."

"Of *The Fire,*" said Stern, naming the illegal newspaper.

"Of *The Truth,*" said the man, naming the single legal publication, voice of the Marshalls.

"Why are you here, then?" said Stern.

"God only knows," said the man; "and the Marshalls."

He dropped the can. It clanked against the metal floor and rolled, trailing a thin bubbling liquid, which widened. Still holding the P-master, Stern shifted until he sat close to the prisoner. He rested his head against the wall and said softly:

"Do you . . . *did* you follow Morgan?"

"Trying to trap me?"

"You're trapped already," said Stern, still softly. "You're for Dispatching. You've got nothing to lose. *Did* you agree with Morgan?"

"Didn't everyone?" said the man, and the past tense melted Stern's stomach.

"You'd give your life for Morgan and *The Fire*?"

"I'm giving it, aren't I?"

The can rolled back, almost empty. Stern stopped it with his boot, lifted it and put it in the rack behind his head.

"You know there are three kinds of Dispatching?" he said.

"So they tell me," said the man.

"You can go screaming; or you can be given a happy pill—which makes you a zombie; or you can get a liberator, which is the kindest . . ."

"You can talk about *kindest* . . . ?"

"A liberator puts you in heaven before you fry or freeze out there," said Stern. "You go home smiling."

"So?" said the man.

"Admit to me you're Morgan, and I'll see you get a liberator."

The man tested the strength of the straps. He sighed.

"OK," he said. "I'm Morgan."

Stern turned his head and looked at him.

"You're not Morgan," he said.

There was a silence.

"How do you know?" said the man.

"I've met Morgan," said Stern slowly. "And no one in the universe could get him strapped on a Dispatcher."

The man smiled.

"But you're here," he said: "aren't you, *Mr. Morgan*?"

And he pressed a button on the center of his black shirt.

The door of the restraint-chamber opened swiftly, and the two guards came in, each holding a Burner.

The man in the straps stopped smiling.

"Get me out of these," he said.

"Yes, sir," said the sergeant.

Stern aimed the P-master.

"I shouldn't worry," said the man, tapping his glowing collar: "this is not functioning."

"I should drop it," said the other guard. "Now."

"What the hell are you playing at?" said Stern. And now the fear was real.

The straps fell back with a faint scraping, and the man stood up. He rubbed his shoulders.

"You walked right into it, Morgan," he said. "Pride before the fall, and all that. You can't combine a lust for promotion with destruction of the system. You should have stayed a humble Captain."

"Who are you?" said Stern.

"One of the nameless patriots," said the man. "Admit you're Morgan, and I'll see you get a liberator."

And he laughed—not nervously like the crew, but richly, and with triumph.

SIX

Stern, alone in the chamber, confined in the straps, a punishment-collar cold and smooth against his throat, waited for Darkness 3 to reach the Dispatching-zone.

The door opened, and the nameless patriot entered. He had changed from prison black to the clean powder-blue of the Marshalls' Corps, and the same fake diamond glittered on his breast.

"I suppose this will make you Colonel," said Stern.

"No doubt," said the Major. "But I'm not concerned

with baubles. Unlike you. I suppose you were intending to infiltrate . . ."

"I'm not Morgan," said Stern.

"Cigarette?" said the Major.

"Bad for my health," said Stern.

"That shouldn't worry you," said the Major, leaning against the wall. "You have about . . ." He looked at his watch. ". . . six minutes."

"Then I'll have one," said Stern.

"Don't try anything," said the Major, and reached forward and lit the cigarette. "Admit you're Morgan and I'll see you get a liberator. Tell me the names of your fellow traitors, and I'll put you off at Cain."

"No, you wouldn't," said Stern. "And I'm not Morgan."

"Suit yourself," said the Major. "We'll get the others, in time. Now that you've gone, the movement will crumble."

"You hope," said Stern.

"We *know!*" said the Major.

As Stern finished his cigarette and stubbed it out on the floor, the door opened once again and the sergeant came in.

"Time, sir," he said.

The Major pushed himself off the wall.

"The others ready," he said.

"Yes, sir," said the sergeant. "All dreaming happily."

"I want Morgan out first," said the Major.

The sergeant gently pressed the button of his P-master. A searing pain shot from Stern's throat to the soles of his feet. It lasted a second, but his body shook in the straps.

"Just a little taste," said the sergeant. "A little warning."
He called to the other guard. "Get him up."

The pain was still there, deep in his bones, as Stern
was released and pulled to his feet.

The Major held out his hand.

"I've been after you for years, Morgan," he said.
"Good-bye."

"No liberator?" said Stern.

The Major smiled.

"No," he said. "I have my instructions. You don't get
off that easy."

Stern stepped out into the corridor. He moved toward
the Dispatcher, a guard on either side of him, armed with
Burners. A line of drugged prisoners waited, their collars
glowing in the blue light. One, more awake than the rest,
lifted his head.

"We going home, brother?" he said.

"In five seconds," said Stern.

The door to the Dispatcher was opened.

"Any last words?" said the Major.

"Yes," said Stern. He turned in the doorway. He looked
at the guards, and then at the Major, and then at the
line of head-down prisoners.

"Now!" he shouted.

SEVEN

The prisoners woke and came alive. They launched themselves on the guards and on the Major, clubbing them
to the ground. One picked up a fallen Burner, and told

the others to stand back. The guards and the Major bubbled, and faded like smoke.

"Go and get the others," said Stern. "Carlson, you stay with me."

As the prisoners ran off, so the big man with the thatch of red hair pressed a fist against Stern's chest.

"It went like a dream, Morgan," he said. "We kept the pills under our tongues, and then we spat them out."

Stern nodded.

"We'll deal with the crew now," he said. "And then it's on to Cain."

"We'll find all we need there," said Carlson, as they moved toward the flight-deck. "Ready and waiting."

"We hope," said Stern, as the Dispatching zone fell back and the far ball that was Cain grew seas and then lands and then earth; and then a thousand uplifted faces.

The Blades

JOAN AIKEN

Right from the start they were enemies. Or at least on opposite sides. Maybe that was to be expected with two boys so diametrically different from each other as Jack Kettering and Will Donkine. Kettering was tall, or tallish, solidly built, with a flat, high-cheekboned, ruddy, handsome face, and a thick crop of burnished red-gold hair. His dad was a Master of Foxhounds, and when the older Kettering came to the school for speechdays you could see just what Jack would become in the course of time—solid, swaggering, red-faced, with his thatch of shining hair turned snowy white. Kettering excelled at all sports—cricket, football, rowing, swimming, athletics; and he was by no means a fool, either; had a knack of learning anything by heart that could be learned in that way, so grammar, mathematical and scientific formulae, dates, facts were always at his fingertips; passing exams was no trouble to him; he was generally among the top four or five at the year's end. He could be funny, too, in a rather unsubtle way, and generous—at least to his friends—he had that sort of air about him which people like Francis Drake and Robin Hood must have carried, so that followers, as it were, flocked to his standard. Not that I mean to say he was an outlaw—oh dear, no. Law-abiding, on the whole, was Jack, more so as he went up the school; of course there was the odd quiet escapade, beer drunk behind the art studios and then whisky in the boat house, dodging off to go to the Motor Show and a night on the spree in London, but these were just schoolboy capers, nothing nasty about them. He enjoyed the reputation of being a good-natured, easy-going fellow. His lot, there were about half a dozen of them, the Blades, they called themselves, were the same kind, and they stuck together all the way up the school.

Later on, when girls were admitted into the upper forms, they all acquired girl friends to match: Kettering's girl was called Pamela Cassell, and she was big and blooming and bossy, with a head of brick-red hair to match Jack's copper-gold, always freshly shampooed and shining and crisp. Captain of the girls' hockey, she was, won the tennis cup three years running, and intended to run a ballroom-dancing school. She had that pink-and-white complexion often found in redheads, and pale china-blue eyes; striking, people said she was, but I couldn't see it myself. If you didn't belong to Kettering's group her eyes passed over you in utter rejection, you might as well have been a garden bench.

Donkine, Will Donkine was, as I've said, in all ways

the complete opposite of Jack. From the start, poor devil, he suffered from his name. Will was short for Willibald, which was a family name; some ancestor had come from Austria—Willibald Edvard Donkine, his full name was, so if he wasn't called the Hun, or Kraut, or Donk, or Donkey, it was Weed or Weedy because of his initials. He came to the school when he was twelve, and by the time he was fourteen the various nicknames had more or less settled down into Donk. Of course it cut no ice at all that his father, Sir Joel Donkine, was a well-known scientist, in line for the Nobel prize. Will Donkine was small and bony, with a pale, hollow-eyed face, short-sighted serious dark-brown eyes (he had to wear steel-rimmed glasses which were always getting broken), and sparse no-color hair like a crop of mousy moss on top of his undistinguished head. Being so short-sighted he was no use at games, and anyway his arms and legs were thin as sticks of celery so he couldn't run fast or catch balls or hit them; he was bright enough, but his wits had a habit of wandering, so that he didn't do particularly well in exams; when he ought to have been answering Question 2, he'd be looking out of the window trying to estimate the flight-speed of swifts, or wondering if it would be possible to turn a Black Hole inside out, or to compress Mars Bars to the size of dice for rapid and economic distribution. His conversation was always interesting—he knew a lot about codes, and ESP, and how people's discarded selves may come back to haunt them (he read books on psychology when most people were reading Biggles) and where you can still find bits of primeval forest in Europe, and what to do if you sit on a queen bee, but his knowledge wasn't very well applied; it never turned up when it was needed. I liked Donkine's company, but he wasn't a popular boy. Part of that was his own fault. He found most people boring; simply preferred his own thoughts. I expect they were more interesting than locker-room chat, but, just the same, if you don't want to have a dismal time at school you need to meet people halfway, display a bit of give-and-take. Donkine did nothing of that kind, so he was an outcast. His solitary state didn't worry him in the least, he spent his spare time reading in the library or measuring things in the lab, or working in his allotment. He was very keen on gardening.

It must be said that Kettering and the Blades gave him a fairly hard time, specially when we were all younger; every now and then they'd rough him up, not *too* much, of course, because they didn't want to spoil their reputation for being decent types; never anything that would show. To do Donkine justice, he never grassed on them; for a day or two he'd go about rather more silent and hunched over, shabbier and a trifle more moth-eaten-looking, that was all. What he did mind was when they messed up his garden; that really hit him in a tender spot. But, as luck would have it, old Postlethwaite the science master was out at three A.M. one night studying a comet and came on Kettering and McGeech systematically digging up Will's artichokes and celeriac, so there was a certain amount of fuss about that, and from then on they had to lay off the garden sabotage; it would have been too obvious that it was them, see? They had to think of other forms of persecution.

While Kettering and the Blades were acquiring girl friends and boasting of their exploits, Will made friends with my sister Ceridwen, who was small and dark and cross-looking. Nothing romantic about their friendship: they were both interested in the same kinds of things. Ceridwen intended to do animal- and plant-breeding later on, and she was very impressed with Will's aptitude for growing things.

By the time we were in the lower Fifth, Will's father had invented his dust extractor, D.R.I.P., it was called, Dust Removal from Industrial and Institutional Premises. Of course it was shortened to DRIP. Don't ask me how it worked—it was a thermonuclear process, radioactivity came into it, and magnetic fields, and the earth's rotation and gravitational pull. Unlike many such processes, it was simple and economical to install. What it did was suck all the dust and grit and germs out of the air inside a building by means of vents on the floor, so that once a DRIP System was installed in your factory—or office block—or hospital—you need never sweep or dust or Hoover or scrub again. There have been similar systems in the past, of course, but expensive to run, and none were so efficient as Sir J. Donkine's. Apparently it really did remove every particle and molecule of anything nasty from the atmosphere so that the air you breathed into your lungs was 100% simon-pure.

Naturally a process, an invention like this was nothing like so sensational as discovering penicillin or DNA or splitting the atom; but still there were articles about it in scientific journals, and old Corfe our headmaster mentioned it in a congratulatory way one morning at Assembly, and said we must all be proud that Sir J. was an Old Boy of our school and his son was our dear fellow scholar, and we must hope that Will would invent something equally useful one day. I noticed Will give a kind of blink behind his glasses at that; he was not at all gratified by being singled out, and I knew why; of course for him it would mean extra hazing and sarcastic broadsides from the Blades for several weeks, till the news had settled down. Old Corfe, who never knew anything about what went on in the school, was unaware of that, naturally; and he was pleased as a dog with two tails about the publicity for the school.

Because of this connection, and before anyone had finished asking "What About Side Effects?" our school, along with several hospitals and a Midland furniture factory, had taken the plunge and had the Donkine DRIP System installed. A demonstration of loyalty it was, on our part, to show our faith and pride in our Old Boy (though I bet that Mr. Corfe managed to get the installation done at half price because of the public interest etc. etc.). Anyway, air vents were set into the floors of all rooms, in corners where they were not inconvenient, and suction pipes, and a big gleaming white tank down in the basement which housed the works. If you held your breath and nobody else was breathing in the room you could just catch the sound of a very faint hum, no more noise than a light bulb makes when it's at the point of death. Nobody could say the DRIP System was loud or annoying. And the school certainly was clean! Not a speck of mud, no dust or fluff could lie on any surface for more than a moment, our clothes and books and bedding and towels all stayed cleaner longer, even substances like spilled jam or glue tended to vanish overnight if not wiped up; and at the end of the first term old Corfe announced with triumph that our health rate had improved by eighty percent, practically no head colds, hay fever, or asthma, and all other infectious complaints much reduced.

The hospitals and furniture factory had reported the same good results; by now Sir Joel Donkine was on the high road to success, fame, fortune, and the Nobel prize. DripCo, the company formed to make the DRIP Systems, could hardly keep pace with the orders; every factory and hospital in the country wanted them now; they were being installed not only in public buildings but also in private homes. Buckingham Palace, if you can call that a private home, was first on the list, and Sir Joel got a decoration from the Palace as well as his Nobel.

What was his son Will doing all this time? Will, of course, had known about his father's intentions long ago, heard the subject discussed since he was nine or ten. His mother had died, when he was six, of an anti-immunity failure, so Sir Joel tended to talk to him a lot when they were together; one of the reasons why Will found most school conversation boring.

Will's main problem after Sir Joel's rise to fame was dodging retribution from the Society of Blades—what they called "necessary discipline" to stop him from getting above himself. *Above himself*—poor Will sometimes looked as if he wished he was under the ground. Most of the Blades, by now, were big and tough as grown men, whereas Will, at fifteen, seemed to have stopped growing for good and was no bigger than a thirteen-year-old. It wasn't for lack of fresh air; he still spent hours every day tending his garden. Unfortunately the school allotments were isolated beyond a row of utility sheds, on the edge of the school grounds; he was much at risk there from the unwelcome attentions of the Blades.

"How's our little Drip today, how's our Weed?" they would say, clustering around him affectionately. "We've come to remind you not to get too stuck-up, just because your dad invented a giant Hoover."

Once they painted him all over with Stockholm tar, which he'd been using on a peach tree he grew from a peach stone; another time they dropped him, and all his tools, into the river; on a third occasion they removed tufts of hair from all over his head. The effect was a bit like a chessboard. That was a mistake, because it was quite visible; old Corfe made inquiries, sent for Kettering and the Blades, and gave them a severe tongue-lashing and various penalties, so their attentions abated for a while.

And Donkine went doggedly on his way, reading a lot, keeping up reasonably well with schoolwork, showing fitful brilliance here and there, specially in chemistry and biology; working in his garden and trying to mind his own business. Whatever that was.

"Don't you ever want to get your own back on those pigs?" my sister Ceridwen asked him once. We are Welsh; I reckon that revenge comes more naturally to us. But Will just shrugged.

"What's the point?" he said. "They'd only make it worse for me, after. You've got to think ahead. And I've got better things to do than conduct a feud. Besides, I have an idea that by and by . . ."

He didn't finish his sentence. His eyes had wandered, as they often did, toward two huge shiny pink potatoes he had just dug up, and a tussock of grass he had pulled out.

One thing he had discovered was that DRIP compost was marvelous for the garden.

I expect you have been wondering what happened to all the dirt and dust that was sucked out of the classrooms and offices and dormitories. It went into black plastic sacks that fitted over the outlet-vents and were removed at regular intervals. The stuff inside them was like stiff dark-brown prune jam, very thick and sticky. Will found that if this was diluted and watered onto the garden, or just spaded around in gooey lumps, like undercooked Christmas pudding, it worked wonders for growing plants. A few weeks of this treatment and Will's artichokes were big as footballs, his spinach leaves the size of the *Daily Mirror* and his roses six inches in diameter.

Postlethwaite the science master (we called him Old Possum, of course, because he had big, wide-apart gentle eyes, and very little chin, and his thin hair wavered backward like water-weeds), old Postlethwaite was absolutely delighted at this link-up between the activities of father and son, evidence of Will's independent research.

"Wonderful work, wonderful, my dear Donkine," he kept saying. "You may have hit on something of real importance there." And he quoted: " 'Whoever could make two blades of grass grow where only one grew before, would deserve better of mankind than the whole race of politicians put together.' Do you know who said that?"

"Swift," said Will without hesitation. But his mind as usual seemed half astray. "People wore wigs in Swift's day, didn't they, sir?"

"We must see if we can't get you the Wickenden award for this," Old Possum went on.

The Wickenden Cup was a school honor endowed by a past rich American parent; it was given from time to time for unusually original schoolwork.

"Oh, *please,* sir, don't bother," said Will, who knew that anything of the kind would only lead to more trouble with Kettering's group. "If you could just ask Mr. Corfe to give an order that the black sacks aren't to be taken away by the garbage trucks but left in a heap here by the allotments. Then everybody who wants to can use them."

But nobody else took the trouble to do so. It's true the stuff did smell rather vile: sweet and rotten like malt and codliver oil.

By and by there began to be odd, apparently disconnected paragraphs in the newspapers: The Queen had been obliged to cancel all her engagements, as she was suffering from a virus cold; a hospital in the north was plagued by an epidemic of ringworm or possibly infectious alopecia; the staff of a Midland furniture factory were all out on strike for some mysterious reason; and the Prime Minister, in the middle of a visit to Moscow, returned to Britain hurriedly and unexpectedly.

Could there be a link between these incidents? The factory and the hospital were two which had been among the first to have the DRIP System installed.

At our school, though, we didn't read the papers a lot; interested in our own affairs, we weren't much concerned with outside news. Time had skidded on its way and by now we were working for our A-levels, up to the eyes in reading and reviewing. Still, even busy as we were, we couldn't help observing something that was happening right under our noses.

Ceridwen, my sharp-eyed sister, spotted it first.

"All the staff are going bald," she said. "Have you noticed?"

It was true. The men's hair was receding at a rapid rate, and the women teachers had taken to various ruses, buns, chignons, hairpieces, to try and conceal the fact that their locks were becoming scantier and scantier. It seemed to affect older people faster, and dark people less than fair.

Then one morning there was a crisis in the girls' dormitory.

Hysterical shrieks were heard coming from the room of big red-headed Pamela Cassell (who by this time was a prefect and so entitled to a room of her own); she had locked herself in and refused to come out. When Mrs. Budleigh the matron finally opened up with a master-key, it was said that she let out almost as loud a squawk as the frantic girl inside. For—Ceridwen told me and Will, then the news spread like lightning through the girls' dorm and so out and about the main school—all Pam Cassell's thick glossy red hair, of which she had been so proud that she let it grow to waist length—all that hair had fallen out in the night and the wretched girl was now bald as an egg, while the hair lay in a tangled mess on her pillow.

Well! What a thing! Needless to say, Pamela was whisked away to a skin and hair specialist; and what he said was so unhelpful that she flatly refused to come back to school, as long as she was such a spectacle, so that was the last we saw of her. Will certainly wasn't sorry. In the old days she used sometimes to stand by and watch while the Blades did things to him.

Meanwhile the mysterious doom struck again: several other people became bald overnight in the same manner, while the hair of others began falling out at a frightening rate. Fair people were much worse affected than dark; I remember watching a blond boy called Titheredge combing his hair one day in the cloakroom, and it was like watching a Flymo go through a patch of hay—three quarters of the hair came away with the comb.

Jack Kettering's was a spectacular case. People from different forms read out the notices each day after Assembly. Tuesday it's the Fifth Formers. Kettering did it one Tuesday; he had a nervous habit, on public occasions, of brushing his hair back with his left hand, and when he did it this time the entire thick reddish-fair thatch fell right off onto the floor behind him. The whole school gasped in horrified amusement and then—reaction, I suppose—a roar of laughter went up. People were rocking from side to side, falling about—how could they help it? The startled Kettering ran his hands over his smooth bare scalp, glanced in appalled disbelief at the heap of hair on the floor behind him, then turned white as a rag and bolted from the school hall.

I noticed that Will Donkine was looking very thoughtful.

"Did *you* do that?" Ceridwen asked him, after Assembly was over. "I mean—did you make his hair fall out?"

Both of us had a lot of respect for Donkine; we could quite believe that he was capable of it.

But—"No," he answered slowly. "No, I had nothing to do with it. Though I'm not surprised—I had an idea something like that was due. And I can't say I'm sorry— when I remember some of the things those big bullies did to me."

He gave a reminiscent rub to his own meagre mouse-brown thatch—which, like everyone else's, was getting noticeably thinner. Ceridwen and I have black hair. It took longer than anybody's to go, but it went in the end.

"No; I didn't do it," Will said. "But I expect I'll be in trouble from Kettering's lot soon enough, if what I think is true."

"What's that?"

"Why, it must be an effect of my father's dust extractor, don't you see? The Queen hasn't been out for ages— they had one in Buck House. And the P.M. had one at 10 Downing Street—and I'm sure she's been wearing a wig for weeks. Have you noticed the newspaper photographs? And then there's that hospital, and the Biffin factory—it'll be all over the country soon, I expect. Father's always a bit too hasty. . . ."

Of course events have proved Will right. A few months more, and all the buildings that had installed

DRIP Systems were populated by totally bald inhabitants.

In three weeks our school, which of course was among the first innovators, couldn't show a single hair among the six hundred students and the forty staff. Even Smokey, the school cat, had gone bald as a pig, and was rechristened Pinky. Even the mice, when seen, could be seen to be bald. Punk cuts, crew cuts, Afro heads, Rastafarian plaits, beehives, all had vanished, like snow-wreaths in thaw, as the poet says.

In a way, our all being companions in misfortune made the state easier to bear. I found it interesting to notice how school relationships and pecking orders had changed and reversed, now that our appearance was so different. At first we found it quite difficult to recognize one another; with no hair, just pale bald scalps, we all looked alike, you couldn't tell boys from girls, we seemed like members of some Eastern sect, ready to bang gongs or spin prayerwheels; and the people who hitherto had prided themselves on their looks went around as humbly as anybody else.

Meanwhile there was a terrific public outcry and fuss. After a while, as Will had predicted, somebody put two and two together and traced the baldness to the Donkine DRIP System. Most of the purchasers of DRIP Systems thereupon switched them off, hoping that the hair of employees, patients, students, and nurses would begin to grow again. But it didn't. Some vital growing hormone, it seemed, had been sucked out for good; or at least, for a generation.

About this time Sir Joel Donkine came back to England from the Brazilian forests where he had been on a research expedition. Naturally he was aghast at what had happened and made a statement about it.

"I accept full blame and responsibility," he said to the newspapers, before his lawyers could warn him not to, and in no time lawsuits and writs amounting to God knows how many millions were piling upon his doorstep.

"Dad's so impetuous," Will said again thoughtfully. "He sounds off without checking the probabilities."

I thought how different his son was. But perhaps I was wrong.

People said Sir Joel ought to have his Nobel and C.B.E. taken away. He was probably the most unpopular man in Europe. What though his System had prevented hundreds of colds and other infections? All that was forgotten in the wave of fury. People marched with placards demanding, "Give Us Back Our Hair!"

Unisex shops and barbers and the manufacturers of shampoos, conditioners, setting lotions, hairbrushes, combs, hairgrips, clasps, nets, ribbons, bathing caps, dyes, tints, and bleaches were all after Sir Joel's blood.

Taken away their livelihood he had, see?

Nobody thought to mention that, on the other side of the scale, makers of wigs, hairpieces, headsquares, hats, caps, hoods, and bonnets were doing a roaring trade. Tattoo artists stenciled ingenious hair designs over people's naked heads, or just drew pretty patterns; colorful head paint was invented; at least part of the population remembered that the Ancient Egyptians went bald from choice, and discovered that there were quite a few conveniences about the bald state.

But as an unusually hot summer drew on there were

a few cases of sunstroke, and questions were asked in
Parliament, and people began to say that Sir J. Donkine
should be impeached, or hanged, drawn, and quartered,
or at least tried for causing grievous public harm.

An inquiry was proposed. But before its machinery
could be set up—public inquiries are very slow-moving
things—poor Sir Joel was dead. Heart failure, the Coron-
er's report announced. And I daresay that was correct.
I'm pretty sure that he had died of a broken heart.

"Poor Father," Will said sadly. "All he wanted was
to help people. He wanted to prevent their getting infections like the one that killed Mother. And so he landed
himself in all this trouble. He never would think before
he acted."

Will grieved very much for his father—the more so
as he had no other relations and would now have to
become a Ward of Court.

After Sir Joel's death, Kettering's group had the grace
to leave Will alone for a while; nobody these days had
the spirit for recriminations. Also we were all working
like Stakhanovites for our A-levels . . .

Will's results in those were fairly remarkable, consider-
ing all he had been through. He came top of our lot,
way ahead of anybody else. And when we reassembled
in the autumn term he seemed in reasonably good shape.
He had spent the summer with Mr. Postlethwaite; the
Old Possum had offered to put him up so he wouldn't
have to go into Care. And apparently he had passed most
of the holidays in biological research.

"Boy's got a really amazing mind," I heard the Old

Possum one day tell Mrs. Budleigh in the cafeteria. "Kind of results he's getting wouldn't disgrace those fellows in the Bickerden Labs at Cambridge. What he's working after, I do believe, is to make up for the harm his father did— or felt he had done, poor man."

"The harm he did seems quite real enough to me," replied the Matron coldly, adjusting her wig. "If the boy thinks he can discover some way of making people's hair grow again, I consider that a very proper ambition."

Will was wholly uncommunicative about his work. Most of it was carried out in the labs—he didn't have time for gardening these days—and it required buckets and buckets of the DRIP System compost that was still piled in black shiny sackfuls by the side of the allotments. He fiddled about with test tubes and cultures and filters, he painted black and brown grease onto mushrooms, and eggs, and frogs, and the bald school mice, and guinea pigs. Ceridwen helped him.

By and by he began to look more hopeful; a spark came back into his eye that had been missing for many months; and, strangely enough, he began to grow, quite suddenly shot up so tall and lanky that he overtopped Kettering and most of the Blades. By now that group had rather fallen apart; two or three of the Blades had left school after their undistinguished A-levels; Pamela, of course, departed after the loss of her hair, and Jack Kettering himself was fairly subdued these days. Becoming bald had changed him a lot. Whereas Will's hair was such a modest crop and unremarkable color that its going made little difference to his looks—indeed, thin-faced, with dark, deepset eyes and newly acquired horn-rimmed glasses he now seemed quite impressive—Jack Kettering without any hair looked flat-faced, florid, and stupid, somewhere between a pig and a seal. And was nothing like so aggressive as he used to be.

Indeed I noticed that nowadays he was cautiously friendly and almost obsequious toward Will, went out of his way to address remarks to him, pass the sugar for his cereal at breakfast, and so forth. Will didn't take much notice, just went on his own way as usual.

One day he captured Pinky the cat (no problem, they had been friends for years) and bore him off to the lab. When next seen, Pinky's pale uncatlike exterior had been dyed all over a delicate rust brown.

"You think the Animal Protection League would approve of what you've done to that poor dumb animal?" demanded Mrs. Budleigh, fixing Will with a sharp gray eye.

"Sure they would; it was done for his own good," Will answered positively. "But if you think it would be better I'll fix him up with an insulation jacket while I wait for results." And Ceridwen helped him construct the cat a butter-muslin jacket, which was sewn up his back so he couldn't get it off. (Pinky showed no gratitude; Ceridwen's hands were quite badly scratched.)

The cat's head was left uncovered and, after a week, anybody gently rubbing under his chin or above his eyes could feel a faint stubble of something growing. This caused a sensation, as you can imagine; people rushed to Will to offer themselves as guinea pigs for his treatment.

Old Corfe the headmaster was down on this.

"Donkine is working hard and I'm sure all our good wishes are with him, but I think it wholly inadvisable that any of the rest of you should submit yourselves as research material, at least without parental consent. We know by now—alas!—what disastrous effects the best-intentioned work may produce."

Anyway it seemed that Will didn't want guinea pigs; he turned away all the people who tapped at the lab door and offered their bald heads for his process.

All but one.

"I've got Dad's consent!" Jack Kettering told him in an urgent whisper. "I phoned home and asked him. He says I look so godawful now that anything could be better. Come on, now, Donk—be a sport! I know I've laughed at you a bit in the past, in a friendly way, but that's all over long ago—isn't it? We're good friends now, aren't we?"

He looked up beseechingly into Will's face. Will said, "You realize it may not be just ordinary hair that grows back?"

"Anything, horsehair, sheep's wool, would be better than having a dome like an egg. I don't care *what* it is, just *do* it, old feller."

So Donkine painted Jack's scalp a rusty brown, and Ceridwen stitched him a butter-muslin skullcap to cover the painted area.

"What's that for?"

"To stop birds pecking it," replied Will gravely.

"Birds?"

"Or anything else. You never know. Wear the cap till I tell you."

Two weeks passed. Pinky the cat's muslin jacket seemed to be getting tight; perhaps he was growing.

One evening as we all sat at supper Pinky hurtled in through the open dining-room window carrying a struggling, cheeping sparrow. The cat had torn his jacket in the chase, it flapped loose, and one of the girls, rushing to the rescue of the sparrow, let out a quack of amazement.

"The cat's gone green!"

"Take off the remains of the jacket," suggested old Postlethwaite.

Ceridwen pulled it off, tearing the tattered muslin with no trouble—to reveal Pinky, erstwhile Smokey, wearing a fine coat of short velvety green.

Someone said in an awed voice, "That cat is covered with *grass.*"

"May I be utterly blessed!" muttered Old Possum. He gazed with bulging eyes at the verdant animal. Will poured the cat a saucer of milk and inspected him with serious satisfaction as he drank.

"It worked with the mice, and it seems to have worked with him. I found it impossible, you see, sir, to grow hair on anything—but grass responded very well—and, after all, it makes just as good a cover—"

Jack Kettering, who had come in late for tea, arrived in time to hear this remark. Without a word, he spun on his heel and strode back into the hall, where there is a big wall mirror, dragging off his muslin cap as he went. We heard him let out a kind of astonished wail.

"Grass . . . !"

Will strolled out after him, and I could hear him say mildly, "You did tell me that anything would be better than having a dome like an egg—"

"I didn't bargain on *grass!*"

But by that time half the school were frothing around Will, clamouring and begging: "Do me, do me, do *me!* I'd *like* grass! Maybe there could be a few buttercups as well? Or a daisy?"

"I shan't do anybody without parental permission," Will said gravely.

I saw him glance, over the clustered shining bald heads, toward Old Possum, with a kind of rueful resigned shrug and gesture of the head. Postlethwaite's expression was still fairly stunned.

"After all, sir," Will went on in a reasonable tone, "you did say that to make two blades of grass grow where one grew before was a good thing to do. And I've made two blades grow where *none* grew before. Think what a hay crop we'd get, off the heads of everyone here."

But I could imagine what Old Possum was thinking, for I was thinking it myself. After grass has been established for a while, you get larger plants rooting, and then larger ones still, and then acorns which sprout into oak trees. . . .

Will was just as impulsive as his father. And who is going to deal with the next lot of side effects?

Zone of Silence

MONICA HUGHES

The sun beat down upon the triangle of desert, and the ancient rocks bore its heat silently. Nothing seemed to move. In the small shadow of a scattering of stones a turtle slept. It opened its yellow eyes to the sun and closed them again.

Beneath the surface the Stranger stirred restlessly. It reached upward, searching for—what was it searching for? Not food, or it could have taken the turtle. Companionship perhaps? But there was nothing out there. Only the overwhelming heat. And silence. The Stranger retreated into the cold loneliness at the center of its being and waited. Sometime. Sometime.

Susan and Dad had been fighting ever since they stopped to gas up the plane at El Paso. The only reason they hadn't been fighting on the flight down was that it was difficult to hear above the noise of the engines. Roger sat opposite them in the airport restaurant and ate his way silently through a dish of tortillas and refried beans. Susan poked at her guacamole salad and talked and talked, while Dad tried to work out his flight plan on the chart in front of him.

"It'll be so boring, Ted. Why don't I stay here until you've finished working in Monterrey? You can pick me up on the way back."

Dad sighed. "That's senseless. The whole point is to go on to Mexico City after Monterrey. We could stay overnight in Torreón if you're really tired. But you'll like the hotel in Monterrey better. Air conditioning. Terrific bar . . ."

Susan traced their route with her finger. "Why Torreón? If we cut across country we'll save hundreds of kilometers."

"I suppose . . ."

"Well, how many?"

"About three hundred. But I'd rather fly by landmarks. Across the desert there's nothing."

"I just don't see the point of renting a plane if all we're going to do is follow the highway down and across. We could have flown a scheduled flight and been there by now. Oh, for a shower . . ."

"Susan, sweetie . . ."

Roger slipped on his Walkman headphones and pushed a cassette into the player. The rich sounds of ABBA drowned out their voices. He sucked up the rest of his milkshake and looked up to see his father's angry face, his moving lips.

"Roger!"

He flipped off the headset. "Huh?"

Susan got up from the table. "I'm going to freshen up." She squeezed past Dad into the aisle, her fingers resting lightly on his shoulders. Long polished nails like exotic seashells. Five seashells, a matched set. Not like his mother's hands.

Roger watched her walk away. The men at the tables she passed stopped talking, however briefly, and their eyes slid around to look at her. He felt mixed pride, rage and shame that someone as noticeable as Susan should be part of his family.

"Roger, will you listen!" He dragged his attention back. ". . . bad manners. Sheer bad manners."

"Gee, Dad, what did I do now?" Then he felt himself blushing, suddenly afraid, though he knew it was ridiculous, that Dad could read the thoughts that ricocheted around in his head whenever Susan was there.

"You do it deliberately, don't you? Plugging into that thing."

"My Walkman?"

"I'm not stupid, Roger. And neither is Susan. You're hurting her feelings, deliberately cutting yourself off from us this way."

"I'm not that keen on listening in on your fights, that's all," he snapped.

Dad stopped being angry and got that apologetic look that made Roger cringe. Dad never used to be like that. "We must all make allowances, old man. There are adjustments in any new family situation. . . ."

"I know. I'm sorry, Dad." He interrupted to turn off the feeble excuses.

Then Susan came back from the washroom and they all went out into the white dusty heat. While Dad did the walkaround inspection Roger and Susan stood by the wing, eyeing each other as uneasily as two strange cats.

The rented plane, a Piper Seminole, was a four-seater. Susan sat beside Dad, with Roger in the seat behind her. The spare seat and the back were filled with Susan's suitcases. Well, most of them were Susan's.

They taxied out and waited in the broiling heat while a 737 took off. Then a DC3. Susan sighed and dabbed cologne on her temples. Dad looked at her uneasily but said nothing.

At last it was their turn. They trundled down the runway, picking up speed. Then the incredible high of takeoff, leaving the weight of everyday life back on the ground. It got to Roger every time. Dad too. He could see his face relax. Smile.

Dad banked and the white houses of El Paso came up to meet them. Then he straightened out and climbed. Roger looked between the seats at the instruments. Just a few degrees off due south.

The sky was a blue glass dish, unblemished from rim to rim. Beneath the plane their shadow crawled over the wrinkled brown earth. The highway between El Paso and Chihuahua was a small thread, clueing them in.

Roger leaned back and pulled out a guidebook that was tucked into the map pocket behind Susan's seat. He flipped the pages idly. A chapter title caught his eye. "The

Zone of Silence." That's what we need in this family, he thought. A zone of silence.

The desert area of northern Mexico, at the junction of Chihuahua, Coahuila and Durango, harbors an electronic vortex that will not permit the propagation of Hertzian waves. There appears to be a magnetic field below the ground the force from which, rising in a funnel shape past Earth's atmosphere, also attracts meteorites and other objects flying over it.

Weird, thought Roger. More Susan's kind of thing than his. She was into articles on UFOs and Atlantis and junk like that. Drove Dad wild.

He put on his headphones and listened to Supertramp with his eyes shut. How was he going to stand the next four years at home? Lord, it would be eight years if he went to university. . . . Why had Dad done it? Why *her?*

"Do you miss your mother, Rog?" Dad had asked, quite casually it had seemed at the time.

Roger had thought about it. Memories of tumbled brown hair and a giggle. Of a game where he hugged her and pretended that his arms wouldn't go around her waist. Stronger memories of good food and always enough socks and underpants in his drawer.

"Yes," he had said to Dad.

It was then that Dad began to talk about Susan. Roger was quite pleased at first, thinking about decent meals and socks. But when Dad introduced her the first thought that hit Roger was: I could never pretend that my arms wouldn't go around *her* waist. Then he had blushed and hadn't been able to stop blushing the whole of that first dreadful evening.

Susan was small and blond and spectacular. And only eight years older than Roger. He'd found *that* out by sneaking a look at her driver's license. After that it became almost impossible to talk naturally to either of them.

He was a numbly polite usher at the wedding, and after the reception had a last comfortable two weeks with the housekeeper, Mrs. Morgan. They had a cozy time tearing Susan to shreds and wondering how Dad could have done such a thing.

"Men!" exclaimed Mrs. Morgan. "It's the Seven Year Itch, that's what it is, like in the Marilyn Monroe picture. He'll live to regret it." Roger had stared at her in admiration, because it was exactly seven years since Mother had died.

Then Dad and Susan had come back, brown and self-conscious from a honeymoon in the Caribbean, and Mrs. Morgan had packed her bags. "Mark my words . . ." she said darkly to Roger as she left. Alone, Roger found himself avoiding both Susan and Dad.

So what were they doing now, cooped up in the cabin of a Seminole, flying over northern Mexico?

It had been Dad's brainwave. "I've got to go down to New Mexico for a consultation. Then a quick trip into Monterrey. Why don't we combine business with pleasure and have a week's holiday in Mexico City? Get away from a Toronto winter. What could be better?"

Almost anything, thought Roger. He changed the cassette. New Mexico had been grim, since *he* was supposed to entertain Susan while Dad was busy. Monterrey would probably be grimmer. Half the problem was that Susan didn't seem to know whether to flirt with him or treat him as if he were ten years old. The other part of the problem, he acknowledged, was in himself.

He glanced past the seats at the instrument panel. Dad had changed course—130 degrees. A bit off southeast. So he'd given in to Susan's badgering and was cutting across country to Monterrey. I hope he knows what he's doing, thought Roger. He looked out of his window. No roads. No small green stains of irrigation. Only the wrinkled reddish brown of ancient land.

Beneath the rocks the Stranger stirred. What had wakened it? A dream of the last visitor? Or perhaps . . . Slowly it gathered its immense power from the cold sad core of its being and reached up, feeling, scanning, like the wavering pencil of a searchlight.

Roger could see Dad's lips move as he talked over the radio. Reporting his change of flight plan, probably. Then his brown hand came into view, fiddling with the dial. He could see Dad's head move as he ran his eyes over the instruments. Well, that was normal. He did it all the time. Once around the sky. Flash across the instrument panel. Back to the sky. Usually casual, relaxed, like watching a tennis match. This time he was edgy. Roger could feel it.

"What's up?" He leaned forward, shouting in Dad's ear. Dad shook his head. Roger could see from the altimeter and the vertical speed indicator that they were losing altitude fast. That made no sense. According to the other instruments they were flying straight and level. The magnetic compass was dithering though. What was going on?

Roger remembered the guidebook. He shouted in Dad's ear. "The zone of silence."

"Not now, Rog."

"But it's in the guidebook."

"I said not now." Dad leaned forward to fiddle with the radio. "I thought . . . but dammit, it's gone."

Susan sat up. "Ted, what's wrong?"

"Not sure." He leaned against her, talking into her ear through her silky blond hair. "I'd have said a whacking downdraft, but we're really too far from the mountains for that to make sense."

"Then what is it?"

"God knows."

"I *told* you, Dad," Roger shouted into the small space between their heads. "It's this place. The radio won't work and it attracts things."

"Like the Bermuda Triangle. Ted, we're going to crash!" She clutched his arm.

"Not if we keep our heads. Susie, don't *do* that. . . . Full throttle and *still* we're coming down."

"Dad, change course. Bear west and get out of it."

"Out of what?"

"The vortex."

"There isn't a vortex. There's nothing on God's earth can pull a plane down, Roger. You know that."

"Then what's happening to us? Dad, listen . . ."

"Sit back, buckle up and shut up. I think I'm going to have to make a landing."

Roger gave up. The red wrinkled land came closer.

The wrinkles became the shadows on the east sides of low ridges. Now he could see individual rocks. A long ridge. Now the ground was rushing beneath them. Another ridge dead ahead. Roger shut his eyes, felt the plane lift, bounce, and come to a stop.

He let out his breath and opened his eyes. Though Dad was a real pain at times he could certainly handle a plane. "Nice work, Dad." He managed to keep his voice steady. He leaned forward to unlatch the door, pushed past Susan and climbed down from the wing to the hot ground.

He stood with his hand against the fuselage listening to the clicking sounds of cooling metal. All around him stretched a vast plain of sand and rock. The highest point seemed to be the low ridge they had just cleared. Roger walked toward it, scrambled up the rocks and looked around.

The landscape was as unreal and empty as Mars. The sky was clear so that not even the shadow of a cloud moved across the land. The plane looked absurdly out of place, like a huge spread-winged albatross.

He could see Dad and Susan standing by the wing, two doll figures. He turned his back on them. To west and north the desert stretched to a saucer-rim horizon. The sun was over his left shoulder, pinning him to the hot ground like a beetle. There was no movement. Nothing lived at all.

Come, begged the silent Stranger. Come, share my cold-ness, my loneliness. It has been so very long since the last one. . . .

A small willy of wind lifted a pillar of sand a meter off the ground and then collapsed. The sand scattered and was still.

Roger's mouth was dry inside. He ran his tongue around his lips. They felt thick and cracked. He turned and began to run down the ridge, his feet crunching against small and still smaller stones and sand, a tiny noise like breakfast cereal. He hurried back to the plane, toward Dad and Susan.

"What did you see?"

"Nothing."

"What d'you mean, nothing?" Susan's voice was high. "There's got to be *something.*"

He had no words for what he had seen and felt. He spread his hands wide, stretched out his arms, dropped them to his sides. "Nothing."

She began to cry. Dad put his arms around her. "It's all right, Susie-love. As soon as I've got the gremlins out of the radio I can get a direction and reset the auto-gyro. There's not a thing wrong with the control surfaces and God knows we've got enough room to take off. We'll be in Monterrey by sunset."

"Promise?"

"I promise." His loving look made Roger turn his back and kick at the tires. "Sit in the shade and relax. I won't be long."

He swung himself masterfully into the cabin. Roger could hear him whistling between his teeth. After a few minutes Roger got up on the step to talk to him. "Dad, it's not going to work."

"Of course it is. Trust me."

"You weren't listening. You never listen now. The guide-book said . . ."

"Hm?"

"It calls this place the zone of silence. It says . . ."

"Nonsense!"

"Have it your way then." Roger jumped to the ground. Susan was sitting in the shadow of the wing, her fingers twisting together.

She looked up. "What does he say?"

"That he can fix it."

"Shouldn't you be helping?"

"Nothing I can do. It's not going to work anyway."

"What d'you mean?"

"I told him before. He never listens."

"Told him what?"

"This." He showed her the guidebook. He'd shoved it into his shorts pocket before the landing. The pages had crumpled and turned in. She straightened them carefully and began to read. Her lips moved.

Roger's anger melted. He shouldn't have shown her the book. It was a cruel thing to do. He tried to take it back, but she hunched away from him and went on reading. At the bottom of the page she stared at him. "It's like I said. Like the Bermuda Triangle."

"Not really." He forced a laugh. "After all we're not drowned."

"Wasn't all this once under water? I read somewhere . . . shells and fossils and things . . ." Her voice died. They both looked across the swell of sand, the wrack of small withered cacti. Her lips trembled. She scrambled to her feet. "Ted. Ted!"

Roger caught her hand. It was warm and moist, with a wrist as small as a child's. "It's just a dumb story. You know guidebooks."

She ignored him and called again. Dad's head appeared at the door. "I can't raise a thing," he said crossly. "Though there doesn't seem to be a darn thing wrong with it. Blast, it just makes no sense." He climbed out onto the wing and jumped to the ground. His shirt had stuck to him, dark patches of perspiration down his back and below his armpits.

"It won't ever work. It says so right here." Susan pushed the book into his hands, stabbing at the paragraphs with her finger. She clung to his arm as he read. Like a person drowning, thought Roger.

Dad read the two paragraphs quickly and threw the book to the ground. "Garbage!"

"It is not. Ted, there are places of power all over the world. Stonehenge. Atlantis . . ."

Dad snorted and Susan dropped her hand from his arm. He eased his wet shirt away from his skin and squatted in the shade. "Hot as hell in that cabin. I'll have another go when it's cooler."

"What's the use? It's not going to work. It'll never work. Ted, we're trapped. . . ." Her voice rose.

The layers of heat seemed to insulate Roger from them. They were like two small actors. From his place in the gallery their voices came to him distantly.

"What are we going to do?"

"Wait till evening. Try again."

"What about food? Water?"

"They'll find us anyway. Once we're overdue they'll check our . . ." The voices stopped. The two small actors stared at each other.

"But you changed the flight plan!"

"You kept on badgering. I said it wasn't . . ."

"Didn't you notify them? Aren't you supposed to . . . ?"

"I was doing it when the radio went out. I don't know . . ."

"They'll never find us. Never."

Roger turned his back on the play and put on his headset. The sun was descending and the shadow of the fuselage stretched eastward. He lay in it, his hands behind his head, listening to the music.

The sun set abruptly. Roger watched the sky darken. The stars shimmered in the heat rising from the desert into the cooler air aloft. After a time they stopped shimmering and shone cold and clear. Roger shivered and climbed into the cabin to get his cardigan.

"What are you doing?" Dad's voice was shockingly loud in the silence. Roger told him. "Chuck down something for Susan, will you?"

He found a sweater, expensive alpaca, silky and warm. The feel of it in his hands made him wonder what it would be like to touch her hair. He dropped the sweater quickly at Dad's feet and walked away, out into the open, toward the ridge of rock.

Then the stars began to fall. Like the end of the world,

he thought, and his heart lurched. But it was only a meteor shower. A real beauty. They skimmed out of the void, flared above his head and vanished. Cosmic fireworks. He lay on his back on top of the ridge and watched until he fell asleep.

Come, the Stranger invited, in a voice so deep that it was inaudible. Share my loneliness. Share my vigil. Come . . .

Their voices woke Roger, Susan accusing and Dad defending. Then she was hysterical and he soothing. So what's new? Roger plugged his ears with music.

The sun was still below the horizon, but, as he watched, the sky turned from deep blue to azure. It was still cool. If there was any moisture in the air at all there should be a dew. One could lick it off the rocks. Better than nothing. He touched them. They were as dry as dinosaur bones.

He began to walk north, away from the plane, along the ridge. It stretched into the distance like the backbone of some enormous prehistoric creature.

The sun popped up into the sky with the suddenness of a squeezed grape. Roger's shadow fell long to the left. He walked on steadily. Music filled his head. When the tape ended he put in another. He never heard the beat of helicopter blades coming out of the east, out of the sun, from Monterrey.

Come, said the music.

Pied Piper

ANN RUFFELL

It took a long time for the fact to sink in.

Not to find no one in the house. It wasn't usual, but just the sort of thing you might expect them to do—get you late for school and therefore punished by someone else. Saves them the bother. Sneaking out leaving no breakfast. He felt annoyed, then defiant. All right, if they felt like that, he'd have what he wanted and as he was late anyway he might as well enjoy himself.

The electricity wouldn't come on, just when he'd arranged the bacon—enough of it for once—in the frying pan. Typical. You'd think they'd done it on purpose. Perhaps they had. After he had eaten he would find the fuse they'd pulled out and put it back in. Meanwhile he spitefully emptied the whole of the remains of a packet of Sugar Frosties—only allowed on birthdays and only in the cupboard because it had been Karen's birthday yesterday—into a vegetable dish and poured a whole pint of milk onto them. It felt great, being deliberately greedy.

Serve them right. They couldn't push him around any-more. They kept trying, as if they never realized he'd been out of nappies for—how long did you stay in nappies? A year?—for thirteen years.

He felt sick. The Frosties? Too much of the little tiger?

Suppose he'd better show up at school sometime. They'd comment if he didn't go. He'd never been ill, not since the usual things: measles, chicken pox, all that. He'd had the lot, and they probably knew there was noth-ing left for him to catch. Unless he had something really spectacular like glandular fever or TB—which he couldn't get, he remembered, because he'd had his BCG only a year ago. All right, lung cancer or emphysema.

No electricity, therefore no tea. Why didn't they have a gas stove? Ridiculous, relying on one source of power. Suppose it never came on, and it got really cold later? Couldn't even chop up the furniture to burn, because there wasn't a fireplace, only radiators. He'd told them before, it was ridiculous. Always get power cuts in the winter. Strikes and that. The only thing they ever had for emergencies were candles, and you couldn't boil a kettle on one of those.

His stomach felt cold. The refrigerator was off, but it couldn't have been for long. There was still ice in the top compartment, and the milk had chilled him. He went upstairs for a sweater. The room was dark. He pulled the curtains.

Nobody.

Nobody outside.

Why hadn't he noticed before? Because down in the kitchen you could only see out to the garden. Up here there was a clear view to the road, normally swarming with traffic, not just at rush hour.

He forced himself to be reasonable. How did he know it wasn't only at rush hour? He was always at school, wasn't he? For all he knew this road was deathly empty like this all the time except between half past seven and nine, or between half past three and six. No, nine. It didn't slacken off until about nine. But during the day, he wouldn't know.

He tried to ignore the fact of weekends, holidays, when he knew it was just as busy. He didn't want to be reasonable about it, in case the reason for this turned out to be unreasonable.

But there was no need for the reason to be at all bizarre. He could think of a dozen reasons why it should be empty. Road works, diversions. He strained his ears for the sound of distant drills and bulldozers. A fly tried, desperately, to escape through the window.

Well then, they hadn't started yet. Had to clear it first.

Or they were making a film. Historical. They had to clear the road of modern vehicles to make way for horses and carriages. Except that the road was lined with palpably modern houses: new red brick, neat box-like garages attached, each cantilevered door painted a different color.

At least a dozen reasons.

Just coincidence that his parents and Karen happened not to be there. It was late, wasn't it? They'd gone to work. Karen had gone to school. Bastards. Leaving him, unwoken, to get into trouble. Bastards.

Forgotten to wind his watch. Even that was against him, he thought bitterly. He raised it to his ear. An ordinary ticking, wind-up watch. They wouldn't buy him a digital, and he had too many other things to save up for.

The watch ticked cheerfully in his ear.

Slow, anyway. Couldn't be only half past nine.

Or perhaps it could.

He grinned, suddenly, his stomach unknotting with relief. Then knotted again when he realized what they'd say when they discovered about the Frosties . . .

No. There wasn't anyone in the house. He'd already looked. They weren't there.

He sat down on his bed and dragged his school sweater on while he thought.

Must be sensible and reasonable about this. Too much imagination, that's the trouble with you. That's what they said at school, with monotonous regularity on his report: "He dreams too much instead of getting on with his work." And then they got annoyed if your imaginative work didn't come up to expectations. No justice.

The radio. He felt a sudden relief. That would tell him what was going on. For Mum and Dad and Karen . . . it was a bit much, to go wherever they'd gone and not tell him, not even *wake* him, even if he did usually refuse. Something as strange as this, not a sound except that fly.

In sudden fury he took a wad of pop magazines and hit the pane savagely, again and again, leaving spattered red and yellow smears as the little crushed body left its life spread on the glass.

Outside a bird shrieked, clattered a warning against a cat.

Not a nuclear holocaust, then.

The radio.

He ran down the stairs two at a time and switched on the radio in the kitchen, the only one that had live batteries.

Nothing.

He could have understood if it was dead. But there was static noise, the conversation of atmospheres. He turned the tuner, gently at first, then with increasing panic.

There was something wrong with it. There had to be. There couldn't be silence from the *world*!

Outside, he yelled at the empty air. He screamed at the road, voicing all the words he knew but had never dared use, demanding a reply. The birds mocked him and then, worse, ignored him. He ran into the middle of the road, flailing his arms, daring a car to course down it and knock him over. In the distance a dog barked, signal for a salvo of yelps and bays and yaps.

Was there somebody there? Someone trying to haul Rover away from the neighborhood canine gang? He ran toward the noise, trying not to see the empty houses. He knew they were empty. There was something about an empty house. It stopped breathing, hibernated, until its owners came home.

Why were they all empty?

Don't stop for an answer, he said, still running. What is Truth? What would jesting Pilate have made of this, then? Did you want the truth?

He turned the corner. The dogs were fighting in the middle of the road, savagely, uncontrolled, over what looked like a joint of meat. Left to defrost overnight in someone's kitchen? He didn't want to go any closer to make sure.

A sob stuck in his throat. You've left me! he screamed. Why have you gone without me? Where are you? Where is everybody?

Mummy!

At the shop, ashamed, he picked up the wire litter bin for ice-cream papers and hurled it violently against the window. He was surprised at the high sound, the small hole that it made in the plate glass. He would have expected the whole lot to shatter.

He didn't even bother to go in. It seemed too much trouble to avoid the broken edges, and there was nothing he wanted, except to find people. No one had come running, angry at the vandalism.

He grew bolder as the morning aged. Thinking stopped him from panicking too much. If they walked out, he reasoned, would they have left their houses unlocked? He tried doors. Surprisingly, they opened. He knocked or rang each time, just in case, but no one answered. He walked inside, tentatively at first then with increasing confidence. He made himself criticize the color schemes, the furniture, tutted like a housewife at the dirt in corners, over stoves, in food cupboards. He tasted leftovers from the dark refrigerators, poured milk for several whining cats, pulled dandelion leaves from an overgrown garden to give to the guinea pig in the house next door.

Not even Breakfast Television.

In another outburst of anger he kicked the screen of

a set concealed in a repro-antique cabinet, in a cozily fake repro-antique room. It imploded silently. No sparks, no smoke. An incongruous twentieth-century mess in an unreal setting.

He had to face the fact, sometime, that he was the only person, probably in the world.

Kayla listened gravely to the Elders. She knew how the procedure went: She had witnessed her father, her mother, do the same task. Now she was of age and responsible enough to make her first decision.

It was very sad, she thought, the way so many developing planets behaved like this. As if they had to strike out, in a childish way, against the Universe, just to prove they were individuals. But they could not be allowed to destroy themselves. Life was not so common, in that sea of matter, that the Guardians could let it be blanked out by accident. For it was by accident really. The babies had found a toy too sophisticated for them to handle properly. Their minds had to be matured in order to use the wealth of their planet fully, and it happened so often that world populations were still at the stage of childish quarrels while their intellects comprehended the edge of all knowledge. They had to be taught gently, lovingly, how to keep their fingers from being burned, how to prevent themselves from being destroyed, just as any children did. They would sulk and stamp, being children, but they would learn, and eventually come to a mature understanding.

But there were some worlds whose inhabitants could not be helped. On the surface they all behaved the same.

It was when they discovered one of the Universe's energies that was potentially annihilating: nuclear power, matter and anti-matter physics, total conversion of matter to energy, the harnessing of black-hole energy—the list was endless. Each discovery could confer greatness on the race that used it. Each discovery was lethal in the hands of a child.

How did they know, then, which children should be guided by the Elders' parental hands, and which would have to be left, sadly, to destroy themselves because they were too dangerous to be left in the Universe?

Kayla answered the Eldest's question diffidently. The smiles of approval from the Gathering were like a thousand suns blossoming from behind an intergalactic cloud.

What was the point of eating, really, if you were going to die?

He shook himself, and threw the chicken leg away, tidily, into the yellow bin on a lamppost. Why are you going on about dying? Why should you die? You haven't yet, have you? Everybody else . . .

But he didn't want to face that question. Not yet.

He still expected to see someone around the next corner. In stories about things ending—there was always someone. It just wasn't possible that he was the only one. Not possible. But then, the whole thing was pretty impossible anyway.

When do I wake up?

The thought that it might be a nightmare cheered him immensely. He would wake up soon, he thought confidently, so he might as well make the most of it. Probably meet a man-eating tiger around by the swimming pool and strangle it bare-handed. Or more likely, knowing dreams, be chased by it and not be able to run properly for the lead in the feet, the unwilling limbs. No. No tigers, please.

There must be someone. He couldn't be the only one. Why him, anyway? Why had he been left? Where were the others?

He had stupid images of millions of people, hypnotized, walking calmly into holes in the ground. Pied Piper. And he the lame one? It wasn't that he was a particularly heavy sleeper. Karen was far worse. She could sleep on a clothes-line through a thunderstorm, Mum always said—usually when trying to get her up in the morning.

Which was why it had been even stranger, them going, when it was Karen more than he who needed a crowbar to get her out of bed.

It would have been nice to put on some music. Desert Island Discs. He could amuse himself looking to see if anyone had a wind-up gramophone and 78 records. He had all the time in the world, years and years on this desert island, with not only the Bible and Shakespeare but whole libraries full of books, his for the taking. Everything in the world was his to use, if he could find out how to use it. By the time he was old and gray he would be quite a little cultural bombshell, all on his own, full of the good things of life yet hardened and capable, used to fending for himself in a hostile environment. He chuckled at his thoughts of solitary heroism.

So long as no one turned up to spoil it.

▲ ▲ ▲

So the world's population was removed out of time, into the shadows of the earth, all except for one: the Contestant.

That person had to be one of those in-between beings: not a child, led by its parents and other adults, nor yet an adult, beginning to be fixed in its ideas and more and more unmoving as it grew older. The perfect time was when the being was in that delicately hovering transition time, having experience of its world but questioning that experience. Only that stage of development was valid, from the Elders' point of view, to assess the potential of a whole species.

"Why?" asked Kayla, though she knew the answer. "Why is there only one?"

"There is never more than one," said the Eldest kindly. "The contest can only be between two people. If there were more than one, it would not be fair."

By evening he was gibbering with loneliness. He hadn't realized it would be quite so bad. It was not the same as being alone: that state you often wanted, feeling oppressed by people around you. But he had no choice. There was too much to do and yet not enough. He hadn't realized how much he had depended on TV, radio, his tapes and records.

He had to search for ways of heating water for a simple thing like a cup of tea. In the end he drank cans of orange, cola, bottles of milk, anything, but felt the need for warmth in his stomach. There wouldn't be milk for long, either: the last refrigerator he looked into had a distinctly odd smell—nothing to do with the electricity being off, but in another twenty-four hours they would all smell like that. Would he get used to cold canned food? There would be enough in the world to keep him going till the end of his life.

Another little surge of fear mocked him. *And how long is that going to be?*

He crushed the thought. They wouldn't last forever, the cans. Didn't they go off, or rust, after a time? He'd have to look it up. Then he'd have to start growing things for himself. Store vegetables for the winter. Would the canned and preserved things last long enough for him to find out how to be self-sufficient? The enormity of it made him shudder. School hadn't prepared him for anything like this.

There were whole fields of crops. What was he fretting about? There were months yet. Plenty of time. Don't worry.

Pity about the milk.

There would be cows, a long way out of town. Why couldn't he drive? Bicycle? He didn't have to come home every night. There were houses for the asking. Home wasn't home anymore, was it?

But he knew he would need to come back to the familiar, just to ease his mind. He had to go back home now, this instant, running down the road past the neat dead houses with his bag of stolen goods bumping his leg. Could you call them stolen when there wasn't anybody to own them anymore? His brain worried, uncharacteristically, over domestic problems which he had never had to solve before. He could throw clothes into a washing machine, cook on a stove liberally supplied with electricity, but without these things . . . ? It must be easy enough. Even Boy Scouts knew how to cook on an open fire. He didn't regret never having been one, nor did he really believe he was incapable of managing.

What about people in airplanes? Spacecraft? Had they been spirited upward, or would they come to land and help him put things on again?

Home.

The familiar scents, the smell of Dad's tobacco and Mum's perfume, garlic and herbs in the kitchen, the faint sour reek of beer fermenting in the larder. Mustn't forget to bottle that at the right time. Were there instructions somewhere? It would be a pity to let it spoil.

He turned his back on the television, resolved not even to try and switch on the radio. Did you make things as normal as possible, or did you start by being different, a castaway, so that the real strangeness didn't show so much?

He began to open a can of baked beans, then put it down half done. He searched among his mother's stores for something totally different, something that was not part of his experience, something that would be more in keeping with his new existence. He rummaged around the shelves, rejecting pilchards, peas, ham, and at the back came across a can with foreign curly script over a picture of what looked like pink tomatoes. In English it told him they were guavas. Perfect.

What on earth did she get them for? he wondered,

spinning the can round the can opener with expertise.
He sniffed, dipped in a finger to taste the juice, chopped
a piece of pink flesh off with a teaspoon and ate.

Could see why she didn't ever use it—though if it was
unopened, how did she know? He grimaced—not so
much at the taste, which was just sweet, like any other
canned fruit, nor even the texture which was a little like
a canned peach but slimier, but the strange aftertaste at
the back of the throat, pungence in the fleshiness.

He turned them into a bowl and sat down, grimly, to
eat them all. If life was to be strange, well then he would
cheat it at its own game and make it even stranger. They
wouldn't frighten him off so easily.

At least, he thought, lighting candles as dusk deepened,
he didn't need to worry about burglars. The thought of
ghosts knocked at the back of his mind but he did not
let it in. Perhaps there would be someone. He couldn't
be the only one. It just wasn't possible.

He locked the doors, in case.

Tomorrow, he promised, pulling up cold sheets to cover
his face, tomorrow I'll go and see.

It was time for Kayla to go. She had been well briefed,
and the Elders had total confidence in her. She could
take time—years, if she needed. It made no difference
to Elder-time, which was reckoned on a different scale,
as human life on Earth was reckoned on a different scale
from a day in the life of a dragonfly. She needed to know
how he would behave in several situations; whether he
would cope calmly and sensibly with his isolation, whether
he would treat other species with respect, whether he

showed that destructive urge prevalent in the adult of the species. If he did not, then the populations could be led back to resume their lives as if they had been in a dream, but with the important difference that those lives would now be protected by the Guardians who would prevent them from destroying themselves. If he did, the world would continue on its self-appointed suicide.

He woke, and sighed with relief. He had never had such a terrible dream, not even those childish nightmares of years ago of which he could remember nothing but the sweating horror of awakening.

He swung his legs out of bed. Sun shone cheerfully through the curtains. It was still early. There was no sound of traffic. The birds argued in the guttering above his window and he heard a cat bleat with desire. He looked at his watch and swore. He had forgotten to wind it again. It said nine thirty, but that must refer to last night. It must be before seven. There was no traffic. . . .

He left the curtains drawn for at least half an hour, not daring to look out. It didn't matter, Mum would shout any minute. There would be the smell of bacon. He could apologize about the Frosties, offer to buy some more.

No. That had been part of the dream.

Don't be silly, there had to be traffic. He only had to look to know it had been a dream. He tugged at the sun-warmed material, wrenched each piece of cloth to the sides in savage handfuls.

"No!" he screamed.

It couldn't be. They wouldn't allow it. It wasn't . . . the nightmare going on . . . on . . .

He tore downstairs, noisy panic in each foot thud. The kitchen was as he had left it last night. The empty guava can on the draining board leered at him. The bread curled in a grin—he had forgotten to put it away. He ran around the house, terrified adrenalin making his legs work like pistons, tearing clothes off empty beds, sweeping away any concealing thing from cupboards just in case— clothes, ironing board, vacuum cleaner, scarves, bags, papers . . .

And stopped, gasping.

Outside it was the same. Empty houses, leering at him. Cars tidily parked. *What had happened?* If there had been a sudden dramatic holocaust the cars would be piled up, heaps of smoking tin. All tidy, all so tidy. Even the halt and the lame and the blind, the old and the babies, not a sign or sound or whisper of a human being except himself.

He sobbed crazily, looking wildly around. He wanted to destroy something. He needed to destroy something, as a punishment for everyone going off and leaving him.

He pulled the bricks ornamenting Dad's flowerbeds out of their sockets, hurled them at windows. He ran blindly into the houses and tore curtains, smashed ornaments, pushed over furniture. He ran back out into the road. The pack of dogs trotted around the corner, stopped and watched him rage, their tongues panting, watching and waiting. He couldn't stand them watching. He picked up one of the fallen bricks and with aimless accuracy hurled it at the leader, a large black Labrador that he vaguely remembered as living at the end house. The pack yelped as he followed the brick with others, but the Labrador lay dead.

The pack scattered, and Kayla stood behind, a girl, about his own age.

He stopped throwing, but a brick stayed in his hand, the arm tense. She looked at him without expression, and his hand moved to his side. The brick dropped to the ground.

In the silence she walked forward to meet him.

He felt sick.

The only other person in the world and it would be a girl and she had to be watching him . . .

There was something odd about her but this didn't occur to him until later. Odd? Not quite right. Not quite . . .

"Hello."

Banal. He tried to smile. The other last person in the world, and that was all he could think of saying. "Are there any . . . have you seen . . ." and then, "I was afraid."

She was close to him now, past the dead dog. The rest had gone yelping away.

"Why?"

The question, direct, was odd too.

"Have you . . . ?" Desperately, wanting to know. "Is there anyone else?"

"No."

So straight, the answer. How the hell did she know? He had thought there wasn't until now, but he had been mistaken. She could be mistaken too, couldn't she?

"How do you know?"

Aha, that stumped her. She didn't answer that one. "How do you know?" he insisted. She had bent to look at the dog, feeling the wound. Ridiculously, he expected a magical cure, that the touch—or a breath, perhaps— would bring it back to life. She stood up.

It didn't.

He took a deep breath to repeat the question for the third time: It was her lack of response that made him angry. Why wouldn't she answer him? The question was harsh in his throat, like sandpaper.

She looked directly into his eyes. Strange eyes, hers. Not like any he was used to. Now that he came to think of it, he didn't normally look into people's eyes, so it could well be that they were quite ordinary.

He couldn't stop his thoughts meandering, driveling. It was all because she was doing this slow-motion sort of thing. Radiation? Something like? Affecting her. The thought calmed him, made her seem an object of sympathy instead of fear or apprehension.

"I was scared," he said again, of the dog. "They were in a pack, coming toward me. I thought they might attack."

He knew she knew he was lying, but it was the best apology he could make. She nodded her head. "Yes." That was all. But she'd agreed to accept his story. He felt normal again.

"Well," smiling the strangeness away, "wonder what's happened? I mean, no people, no corpses, where—?"

"Does it matter?" said Kayla. All at once he felt happy that she was in control. "Where are you going to live? Do you mind if I come with you?"

Suddenly she didn't seem strange anymore. He wondered why she ever had. Because everything else was, no doubt. They'd get used to each other.

He lost track of time. He realized when leaves began to drop that he had no idea of the date, whether it was an early autumn or a late one. He had done a lot of thinking and reading. He felt he had been quite resourceful in many ways. He felt keenly his appalling lack of knowledge in too many others. He was comforted by Kayla's help and confidence in him, the way they worked together as a team. He still had wild bouts of anger—mostly when he was feeling frustrated: He couldn't do something or he had to wait for a result. He felt she understood. He was occasionally angry that she seemed so lacking in anger. And yet she wasn't cold—not at all.

They had gone out to the country, found an attractive cottage—there were cows and goats and hens—begun the lonely, semi-agrarian life sentence. And yet he enjoyed it, the necessity to tend the animals, day in day out, no one else to do it for him. He tinkered with farm machinery in the fields a couple of miles away. He learned the rhythm of days, grew close to the earth with its predictable and unpredictable moods. The winter came and went. His muscles grew stronger and his brain sharpened. It was no longer so difficult to do things.

It was autumn again. They had harvested what they could, stored anything that could be stored—he hoped they'd done it right; some of the articles in farming magazines were so technical. Well, there was still plenty of canned and preserved stuff left if they hadn't.

He watched Kayla through the window. A trick of light? Too many cobwebs? Floating over the grass in the orchard? He blinked. Her feet were planted in the grass, walking firmly back. The last few leaves on the small plum nearest the cottage rattled on the glass pane in a gust of wind.

She joined him in the kitchen.

"I think we'd better go back to town, to your house."

He had had the urge himself recently, and wasn't surprised.

"Take everything, or just for a day or two?"

"I'll get things," she said. "Don't you worry."

As the people slid out of the shadows, blinking as if out of a pleasant dream, Kayla returned to the Elders, bearing her verdict.

He wriggled his toes in the familiar bed and felt the sun already hot behind the curtains. There was the noise of traffic outside, not too loud, just enough to remind him there were people—suckers—getting up and going to work.

As he ought to go to school.

He smelled bacon as he dressed and heard the eight-o'clock news as he went downstairs. Another revolution, somewhere; more missiles; rows about dumping nuclear waste . . .

He shook a dream from his head and went down to another day.

Hally's Paradise

DOUGLAS HILL

Hally Kenner paused at the top of a low rise, took a deep breath of the cool air, and gazed around at the landscape, as he had done several times that morning.

It's ideal, he thought, as he had also done several times that morning. *A fine planet. A fine place to live, and to die.*

He strode away down the slope, through thick, knee-high brush and out onto a sweep of open land covered with a purplish growth that was more like moss than grass. Its soft springiness under his boots made him feel more light of foot than he had felt for years. For, although he was lean and straight-backed, Hally's hair was gray and thinning, and his face was deeply lined by some sixty years of a hard and dangerous life.

But he had left that life behind him, now—to start a new life, on this planet. This ideal planet.

He knew that most other people would not have found

it ideal. They would have used words like bleak, and dull. The rolling plain of moss seemed to go on forever, interrupted only by swathes of the thick, feathery brush, like ferns—and by an occasional range of low, bare, rock-clad hills. The place even lacked any interesting life forms, to break the monotony. The largest creatures Hally had seen looked like slugs covered with shell, half a meter wide, slow-moving, entirely harmless.

But all the things that would make the planet seem dull and empty and boring, to most people, were the things that made it ideal for Hally. He had had enough excitement and danger in his life. Now he wanted just what he had found on this world—silence, and emptiness, and peace.

But as he strode along over the rich moss, the silence was broken—by a snuffling sound from a cluster of brush nearby, followed by a hoarse coughing like a human with a heavy cold. A smile tugged at the corners of Hally's thin-lipped mouth. *I'm not the only one,* he thought. *Skitter thinks this place is ideal too.*

Skitter was a creature called a *wiryz,* from a planet on the far side of the galaxy. He had been Hally's faithful companion since the day Hally had found him, a tiny, abandoned cub. Now, fully grown, Skitter was a thigh-high bulk of gray fur and muscle, with a long triangular head that displayed two pairs of eyes and a mouthful of sharp black teeth, serrated like a saw. He also had eight legs, like every wiryz, and moved in jerky, high-speed bursts that had given him his name.

Hally's smile broadened as he heard Skitter's cough deepen into a resonant roar. That roar, combined with the solid bulk and the sharp teeth, could make a wiryz seem fearsome. But in fact the creatures were vegetarians, not hunters, and certainly not fighters. Skitter was gentle, playful, good-natured, and a complete coward.

Just then, Hally guessed that Skitter was trying to play with one of the slug-things, which would be ignoring him totally. But if the slug showed the slightest sign of aggression, Hally knew, Skitter would turn and run as fast as his eight legs could carry him.

For an instant Hally glimpsed the big creature, charging through the brush. As always, when he was happy, Skitter's mouth was gaping wide in a foolish grin that exposed all of his shiny black saw-teeth. For Skitter, who had spent much of his life cooped up in spaceships, all this wide-open land was clearly a joyous paradise.

And for me too, Hally thought, *it's as near to paradise as I could find.* But that, he knew, really had little to do with the nature of the planet itself. It had to do with the total absence of other people.

Hally had known a great many people in his life. But he had liked few of them, and had loved none. And in the end he had come alone, except for Skitter, to spend the last years of his life on a planet that offered him peace, not people. Because peace was something that Hally Kenner had almost never known, through all his sixty years.

In his youth, Hally had been a drifter, wandering from planet to planet of the League of Human Worlds, looking for adventure. He had found plenty of that—but he had also found, on all of those colonies, that people were still people. Wherever they went in the galaxy, they took with them all the old human failings, all their greed and fear, envy and ignorance. And wherever Hally went, in all the hundreds of planets of the League, he found the same old human drift toward ugliness, misery, destruction, violence.

What was perhaps worse, Hally had found that he too had the human capacity for violence. And the skills that went with it had come swiftly and easily to him. So his own drifting had led him, almost naturally, to earn his living with those skills—as a mercenary soldier.

Over the years, his reputation had grown and spread, throughout the League of Human Worlds. And when the League had finally fallen apart, in a welter of corruption and treachery, the mercenary warriors of those planets came into their own. The catastrophic Wars of the League had shattered humanity's dream of colonizing the galaxy. But they had made the name of Hally Kenner into a legend.

Yet Hally had gained no satisfaction from his fame, or from the use of his fighting skills. He had fought to earn his living, because it was the thing he did best. But all those years of destruction and death had turned him grim and bleak and cold, sickened by what mankind was capable of doing to itself. And so, finally, he had got out.

He had used all his savings to buy and equip a small space cruiser. And then he and Skitter had set off for the farthest reaches of the galaxy. His plans had formed so completely in his mind that it was as if they had always been there, waiting for him to notice. He intended to find an uninhabited planet, far from the Human Worlds, and spend the rest of his life on it, in peace.

And when he had wandered into this region, and had found this planet, it seemed as if it too had been waiting for him.

It was called Gammel V on the star charts. It was chill and bare and empty, but able to support human life. It was the kind of world that the League might once have colonized. But the League was now in ruins, and humans would be doing no more colonizing for a century or more—by which time it would no longer trouble Hally. So he had landed his ship, on a patch of solid rock within one of the ranges of low hills.

The landing had been the day before, and he had spent the rest of that day taking what he needed out of the ship. He had brought a small dome-shelter of pre-fab plastic, solar-powered recycling equipment that provided food and water, and a few other items—including his nova-gun, the only weapon that he had packed. He had carried all that equipment out onto the rolling plain, and had set up his home in a gentle fold of land, about two kilometers from his ship. And then, this morning, he had come out to look at his surroundings.

He and Skitter each had years of life left. And he was sure they would be good years. He could already feel peace settling around him, in the absence of people, with their uglinesses and violence. And he would not be bored. He would think, and dream, and play with Skitter, and wander—and it would be enough. He had a whole world to investigate and explore. His world.

I came looking for a hermitage, he thought wryly. *And I found a paradise.*

▲ ▲ ▲

By midday Hally had circled halfway around the perimeter of the low hills where he had landed his ship. The walk had given him an appetite, so he decided to return to his dome-shelter by crossing over the hills, and along the way taking another look at their bare, rocky ridges and the gravelly clefts between them.

Soon he had climbed easily up one of the steeper slopes, and was angling downward into a dusty gully. As he walked along it, the gully deepened, its far side becoming an almost sheer wall of low cliffs. Hally felt pleased. The cliff walls would offer the enjoyment of a little rock-climbing, and they were also split and broken here and there by the gaping dark mouths of caves, just waiting to be explored.

But there was no hurry. He could come back next day, or next week. He could explore every centimeter of the gully, and all the others like it among the hills. It could take him months, maybe a year, if he went about it slowly and thoroughly. And that thought made him feel even more happy and peaceful.

But then, as he moved around a bend in the gully, he stopped short, breath hissing between his teeth with shock. And almost all thought was driven from his mind.

Ahead of him, in the cliff-face, was the entrance to another cave. And in that opening stood something that told Hally he was not the first space-traveler to have landed on Gammel V.

A statue.

It was about a meter and a half high, sculpted from a substance that was rough-textured like stone, but gleaming like metal. Clearly it had been there for a long time, so that wind and weather had had their eroding effect on the surface. But there was more than enough to show Hally that it had not been carved by humans.

It was a statue of a being of some sort. Vaguely humanoid, with two thick legs, a long narrow torso, four multi-jointed arms, a head like a large oval lying on its side. The arms were upraised, and the head was tilted up toward the sky. And the broad feet rested not on a plain pedestal but on a carving of a machine of some sort. It was vaguely a hemisphere, with strange protuberances sprouting from it. And Hally felt certain, though he could not have explained why, that it was some kind of spacecraft.

A light wind moaned around him as he stood in the gully, rooted, amazed, staring. And as he stared he shivered, not from cold but from the eerie feelings that the statue caused within him.

Humans had found only a few other intelligent species among the stars. All of them had been at more primitive stage of development, without spaceflight. And none of them had looked anything like this sculpted figure.

Again Hally shivered. It was not just the alienness of the statue, nor its obvious great age. From it came a feeling of dignity and strength, but also a terrible loneliness, a deep, soul-wrenching sadness. It affected Hally much like some objects he had seen on old Earth—broken statues of ancient gods, crumbling memorials to long-forgotten heroes. But this statue was more awesome, because it was more mysterious.

In the distant past—perhaps before humanity had come out into space—alien beings must have passed this way, left this statue, and then departed. What they were, where they went, why they had left the statue—these were mysteries that Hally knew he would never solve.

But then, as he stared at the alien sculpture, another thought entered his mind. An unworthy thought, but a very human one. A temptation.

Back on the Human Worlds, he knew, there were museums and wealthy people who specialized in collecting artifacts from alien planets. Such artifacts were often worth a great deal.

And for this statue, with all the mystery of its origin, a man could literally name his own price.

He stepped slowly forward, letting his fingers slide over the harsh surface of the sculpture. If he were to take it back and sell it, he would be rich. As rich as any of the Lords of the Nebulae. And then he could . . .

Abruptly he turned away, shaking his head angrily. Without looking at the statue again, he stalked rapidly away along the gully, as if trying to get away from the temptations that the alien object presented. But as he hurried on through the hills, those thoughts continued to clamor in his mind. Thoughts of great wealth, unending luxury for all the years that were left to him.

The dream of living out his life on Gammel V, alone and in peace, faded away. Part of his mind was telling him that a spartan life on a bleak deserted planet was no life for a tired old warrior. Far better, his thoughts were saying, to find comfort and rich pleasure, on one of the lush resort planets untouched by the Wars of the League, attended by servants, surrounded by all the delights that wealth could buy. And all he had to do was to load the statue into his ship and take off.

Such thoughts were still swirling and whispering in his mind as he came down out of the hills, on the far side. He was half jogging now, as he crossed the two kilometers of rolling mossy plain to the cleft of land where his dome-shelter stood. But though his mind was clouded by the temptations, lost in dreams of wealth and luxury, he was still Hally Kenner, with all his lifetime of training and battle-hardened skills.

So as he approached his little dome, he stopped suddenly, hairs on his neck prickling with the reflex awareness of danger.

Something had been tampering with the dome. He had locked its narrow door out of habit, and only his thumb-print could open it. But the plastic around the lock was deeply scarred and gashed, as if something had been trying to break in. And the gashes looked like they had been made with knives, or claws.

He wheeled slowly, in a balanced crouch, studying the empty landscape, grimly wishing that his nova-gun was not stowed away inside the dome but clipped to his belt as it had always been for so many years. The thick brush on the slopes around the dome seemed to have become dark and ominous, as if it were hiding a host of unseen, unknown enemies.

And then he froze, rigid as if he too had become a statue carved from stone. Behind him he had heard the

one sound he had thought he would never hear again.
Another human voice.

"Stay where you are, old man," the voice said, in a
rough growl, "and you won't get hurt."

Though Hally remained blank-eyed and unmoving, a
mixture of emotions swept through him like a storm.
Shock, wariness, a clear awareness of danger, and a sudden clench of shame that he, of all people, should have
walked into an ambush. And with those feelings came a
cold swelling anger, and outrage.

It was bad enough that a stranger should have taken
him by surprise. It was far worse that any stranger, any
other human, should be there at all, on Hally Kenner's
world.

Ignoring the voice's order, but keeping his hands mo-
tionless, Hally turned, slowly and carefully.

He saw three men, in stained and crumpled coveralls,
stepping out from behind the far side of the dome. Each
had a nova-gun on a belt-clip, and one also had a heavy
knife jutting from his boot. They were standing well apart
from one another, to make three separate targets. Hally
knew that if he lunged at them, bare-handed, he would
probably get only one before the other two fired. Twenty
years ago, he thought sourly, I might have got two—but
the third would kill me just as dead.

None of these thoughts, none of his flaring emotions,
showed on his face as he stared at the three men.

"Saw your ship land yesterday," the man in the center
said. He was the owner of the rough voice, probably

the leader. Heavily built, coarse features made coarser by smears of dirt and several days' growth of beard. "Took us till now to get here," he went on, grinning. "Nice place you made for yourself."

Hally said nothing, just watched them stonily. He knew their kind well enough. A trio of drifters, probably criminals wanted on several planets. What ugly mischance had brought them here?

As if aware of the question in Hally's mind, the leader of the trio answered it. "Our ship came down a few days ago. Malfunction—useless. Figured we were stuck on this ball of nothing forever. Real nice surprise to see you coming down. What I can't figure is what you're *doing* here."

"Who cares?" one of the others said sharply. "Where's your ship, old man?"

Still Hally said nothing. And the leader shifted one hand slightly toward his gun.

"We'll find it, sooner or later," he said. "But you can save us some trouble—and stay alive—by telling us."

Hally knew that the trio would kill him at once without a second thought. So he jerked his head slightly, toward the hills. "Over that way. About two kilometers."

"Good," the leader said, his grin widening. "Now you can step over here and open up your dome, so we can see what else you got."

Hally's mouth tightened, but again he knew that he had no choice. He stepped forward, watchfully. And as he did so, the leader's eyes narrowed.

"I got the feeling I've seen you before," he said. "What're you called?"

"Hally Kenner," Hally said quietly.

He saw the slight widening of the eyes, the tensing of the jaw, on all three men. Clearly they knew the name, and the reputation that went with it. But then the leader's grin slowly returned.

"Course," he said. "The great Hally Kenner. I was in one of your star troops one time—must've been fifteen years ago. Just a kid then, I was, a recruit. You remember? Creel's the name, Lann Creel."

"No," Hally said with blunt honesty. "I don't remember. But I don't think you'd have been in my troop for long."

As one of the others snickered, Creel's grin became a snarl. "That's right. You chucked me out, for stealing." His laugh was vicious and ugly. "And here we are, and I'm still stealing. Only it's your ship, now. And you can sit on this nothing planet for good, Mister Hally Kenner, and think about the old days . . ."

But then the tirade stopped—because it had been interrupted. By a hoarse, coughing roar.

Over the top of the slope at one side of the dome, Skitter came lolloping on his eight wiryz legs, glittering black saw-teeth exposed in one of his most foolish grins.

Automatically, all three men whirled toward the unexpected sound. They saw a huge gray-furred beast, fanged mouth gaping, charging toward them with a terrifying roar. Instantly their hands flashed to the nova-guns at their belts.

But just as instantly, Skitter skittered. With all the awareness of a true coward, the wiryz sensed the fear and aggression in the three humans even before they had touched their guns. Wild panic turned Skitter into a fleeing, eight-legged blur. And the three nova-rays seared harmlessly through the air as Skitter vanished back over the top of the slope.

"What in starfire was that . . . ?" one of the men began.

But he was interrupted by a vicious curse from Lann Creel, the leader. Creel had swiftly swung back toward the gray-haired man who had been standing silently before them.

But Hally Kenner was no longer there.

In the fractional second that the men had taken to turn, see Skitter, and fire, Hally had simply vanished. There was no sign of him, no sound of his movement, anywhere around.

"Come on!" Creel yelled wildly. At a headlong run, the threesome dashed away up the other slope, in the opposite direction from Skitter.

And, lying full length in the thick brush nearby, Hally listened to their departing footsteps, with a small cold smile. When Skitter's arrival had given him the chance he needed, he had simply taken three swift strides and dived head-first into the nearest cluster of the fernlike brush. Then he had slid away, bellydown, with a stealth that did not rustle a single feathery leaf, through the shadowy heart of the dense growth.

As he lay there, listening to the fading sound of three pairs of running feet, he heard a low snuffle behind him. Turning his head, he saw Skitter, all four eyes wide and fearful, edging nervously toward him. He reached out to stroke the rich gray fur, feeling the wiryz's trembling sub-side.

"Still," he murmured. "Still."

Obediently Skitter lay down, tucking his legs under him. The brush would keep him hidden, Hally knew, even if the three men doubled back. Which was not very likely.

"Stay still," he told Skitter. Then he rose and moved toward his dome.

A moment later he emerged from it, his nova-gun clipped to his belt. And there was a cold glint in his eyes, like the sun on ice, as he climbed warily up the slope, toward the hills where his spaceship stood.

He moved with instinctive care, making full use of the natural cover on the brush-covered slopes, then of the even better cover among the jutting stony ridges of the hills. Yet he moved at speed, in an easy lope, drifting across the terrain like a shadow. He was hardly aware of how all of his old skills had come smoothly into action. What he was doing was simply second nature to him, using the abilities that had kept him alive through hundreds of similar pursuits, through hundreds of other alien land-scapes.

Several minutes later he was tucked into a rocky crevice on one side of a broad, flat plateau. In the center of that open area his cruiser rested on its landing gear, angled upward, pointing at the sky. The three men had not yet reached the plateau—but within moments Hally heard their approach, heard their voices from a nearby cleft.

"I still think we should've stayed and looked in that

dome," one of them was saying. "It could've been full of good stuff."

Lann Creel's reply was a vicious snarl. "You want to go back, with Hally Kenner out there somewhere, you go ahead."

"He's an old man, Creel," the third one said. "We could've hunted him down—there's three of us."

"Old, maybe," Creel spat. "But he's still Hally Kenner. You saw how he disappeared. We'd never find him, if he didn't want to be found. And then it'd get dark, and he'd come and find *us*. Remember, I've seen what he can do. So we'll find his ship, and get out of here while we still can—and be glad of it."

The sound of his voice had grown louder, as the three men had drawn nearer to the plateau. And then Hally drew back into the crevice, for he had seen them— crouching at the edge of the plateau, staring nervously around, no more than thirty meters away. But clearly they saw nothing except an empty expanse of bare rock, and the silent spaceship in the center.

"There it is," he heard Creel say. "And it looks like we got here first. But he'll be coming after us, probably with a gun. Let's move."

Hally heard their boots crunch on rock, and edged carefully forward. The three were moving out on the plateau now, heads twisting around as they kept a wary eye on the barren rock around them. Silently Hally raised his gun, sighting along the bulbous barrel. In their nervousness the trio had bunched together, and he could drop them with a single fiery blast.

His finger began to tighten on the firing stud. He felt no scruples about killing from ambush. Killing was killing, neither heroic nor admirable however it was done. And he was coldly, grimly ready to finish off these men. They would have murdered him just as readily, he knew. And they were trespassers, intruders into the perfect peace and emptiness of his ideal planet.

But then he hesitated, lowering the gun, as a new thought came to him. If he fired, the men would *still* be intruders. Their corpses would be there, on the planet, even if Hally buried them as deeply as he could dig. He would always be aware of them, as other presences that did not belong, shattering his isolation.

And at that moment the realization of what he was thinking jolted him, like a physical blow.

Ever since the three men had appeared, he had not given a thought to the alien statue in the cave. He had not even felt a second's worry that the trio might discover the statue, and take it from him. Nor had he been even briefly troubled by the threatened theft of his ship.

His anger and outrage, his cold determination to kill, had been caused solely by the fact that the men were *there,* intruding on his paradise.

Slowly, with amazement, he shook his head. He recalled all those dreams, of wealth and luxury, that had entered his mind as he had stood staring at the alien sculpture. What had been happening to him at that moment? How could he, Hally Kenner, have ever thought such thoughts, felt such insane temptations?

Great wealth might bring comfort and luxury, but at a price far greater than money. Hally had met many rich people, and had found them all to be empty, greedy and fearful. Empty because they acquired things too easily, and so drew no pleasure from them—greedy because they always wanted to acquire more—fearful because the Worlds were full of dangerous folk who wanted to take the things of the rich away from them.

He shook his head again. How could he have thought that he could ever go back among the worlds of people, where he would find nothing but violence and ugliness, and a rich man's self-indulgence? How could he have dreamed that there would be contentment and peace in a life like that?

He suspected that even if he had given in to the temptation, he might have come to his senses sometime. But by then it might have been too late—he might have been too old, too weakened by soft living, to make a real life for himself on a world like Gammel V. So, in a way, the three intruders had done him a service.

Smiling a thin smile, he looked across the plateau, at the three nervous figures who had now almost reached the cruiser.

You can have the ship, he said to them silently. *I'll have the planet. And I've got the best of the bargain.*

He watched without moving as the trio hastily fumbled for the outer control to the airlock, then scuttled into the ship. Within seconds a spume of fiery gases burst from the ship's stern—and within minutes more the cruiser was lifting from the plateau on an eruption of flame, howling up into the cold blankness of the sky.

Still and silent as the rock around him, Hally watched the ship climb until it disappeared. He felt no sense of loss, since the ship would be of no further use to him. And its theft removed any chance that he might, at some later time, give in to the temptations that the statue offered. He felt almost grateful to the three thieves.

And he felt such overpowering relief that they were gone from the planet, that he would not have minded if they had taken all his possessions.

Of course, he thought, they might come back, and try to steal the rest of his equipment. But he doubted it, since they had been in such a towering hurry to get away from him. And if they *were* stupid enough to come back, he told himself firmly, they wouldn't take him by surprise a second time.

Nor was there much chance that they would tell other people in the Worlds about finding Hally Kenner alone on a distant planet. Too many questions might be asked, about *how* they had found him. And the questions might uncover their theft of the ship, and the fact that they had left him there, apparently marooned.

He clipped his gun back onto his belt and turned quietly away, heading back toward his dome-shelter. First of all, he intended to call Skitter out of his hiding place in the brush, and to reassure the wiryz that all was well, that the danger was gone—that there would probably never be any more danger for either of them, ever again.

Then we'll go and have another look at that statue, he decided, as he strode peacefully along. *And tomorrow, we'll go for a really long walk, and look at some more of our world.*

Our paradise.

Program Loop

JILL PATON WALSH

The summer he was sixteen Robert's parents left him alone in the house for three weeks. His father was going to New York on business, and his mother needed a holiday, and wanted to go with him. Robert had had glandular fever; think of something for a boy to do, and he couldn't do that, because he needed rest. He just had to stay put and bear it. His mother stocked the freezer lavishly, and wrote instructions on postcards taped all over the house, before getting on the plane, a day before his dad, through some mix-up over tickets.

"Even convicts don't have solitary confinement except as a punishment," said Robert, but only to himself. Then, on the last day, Robert's father bought him the computer.

"I thought it might help to while away an idle hour," he said, putting the machine, leads dangling, on the kitchen table.

Robert's eyes widened. "That's brill, Dad!" he said.

"Mega-amazing! But can we afford it?" In spite of trips to New York, Robert's father worked in a field that was all glamor and not enough cash.

"There's a lot more of it," his father said. "Give me a hand getting it in from the car. Where do you want it?"

There was indeed a lot more of it. A very good monitor, better than a TV set. A disc drive. A box of discs. A printer. Fanfold paper. Leads, the user manual. The disc drive was huge: 800K.

"But *can* we afford this?" Robert said, as they laid it out on the desk in his father's den.

"For my boy, nothing but the best!" his father said. "No, truth is, Robert, it's all secondhand, and I picked it up very cheap. Astonishingly cheap. As if the man wanted to sell it to me in particular. So it's all yours, and don't worry about the money."

"Imagine having all this, and wanting to sell it!" said Robert. "It looks new."

"Well, I didn't actually meet the guy who had used it. Bit odd, in fact. He seems to have disappeared, and his father is selling up. Our good luck. Do you know how to use all this?"

"I've never had my hands on one of these before," said Robert. "It's very new and advanced. Supposed to be the absolute best. But I expect I can manage."

"Good. Good. Well, I've got to pack."

Robert spent half an hour getting all the cables plugged in and everything connected together. To connect things to the mains he needed one of those floating sockets that takes four or five plugs, and needs only one plug in the mains; there was only one power point in his father's den—the one his mother used for the vacuum cleaner. And he didn't like to go and buy one till he had seen his father safely off—it didn't seem friendly.

So one way and another it was the following day before he really settled down to work on it, and he had already had a long evening in front of the television set, and the amazingly dislikable experiences of going to bed without anyone to say good night to, and going out shopping without anyone to whom to say "Just popping down to the shops . . ." He had every intention of getting lost to the world with his new machine.

Getting it up and running proved easy enough. It might be secondhand, but it was in perfect order. The previous owner had left not so much as a smudgy fingerprint on a key, never mind any little snags to correct. Robert summoned up the BASIC he had learned at school, and began to play. First he made it print **HELLO ROBERT YOU GENIUS** on the screen, flashing on and off. Then he made it draw the diagram for Pythagoras' theorem. Then he started on his own great project—writing a program to make it play bridge. This was really an interesting job. You had to make the machine divide fifty-two signs, one for each card in the pack, into four "hands" completely at random. Robert got a bug in his program, and the machine kept making hands that repeated cards in one of the other hands. Obviously, he had to sort that out before he taught it scoring and bidding. . . .

Eventually he realized he was not just hungry, but *rav-*

enous. It was six o'clock, almost suppertime, and he hadn't bothered with lunch. No wonder. No Mom, bringing sandwiches, or saying, "Robert, you must eat." Robert winced. He honestly hadn't expected to miss his mother. He had expected to be glad to see her when she got back, but actually missing her . . . Oh, well, live and learn.

But he was in a dilemma. The machine was quite warm now, having been run all day, and Robert thought it would be better to turn it off while he made and ate supper. But if he turned it off he would lose the bridge program unless he managed to "Save to disc," and he hadn't yet mastered the disc drive. But he was *very* hungry. He switched the drive on, and put one of the old owner's discs into it. "**SAVE 'BRIDGE' TO DISC**" he typed.

DISC FULL came up on the screen.

Robert scrabbled through the manual, and typed "***ENABLE. *ERASE.**"

ERASURE PROHIBITED said the screen.

"Hell!" said Robert, and tried another disc. The third he tried seemed to be empty, and he stored his program safely on it, switched off, and got himself into the kitchen. A pork chop? No, takes time to cook and doesn't look too good to eat raw. He concocted a sandwich of pilchards and peanut butter, topped it up by eating a whole drum of ultrarich American ice cream, and promptly fell asleep on the sofa in front of the television, until the piercing close-down tone woke him up. He seemed to have indigestion, so he made himself hot cocoa, using milk that had been standing on the doorstep all day and tasted a bit funny. The cocoa had floaters in it, but it was warm, anyway.

At least he was learning the value of breakfast. The bridge program kept him going through lunchtime day after day. He needed books, too. He went to the computer shop to buy them. And while he was there he noticed, on a price list for discs, the brand name, unknown to him before, of the ten discs that had come with the machine. Eight pounds fifty each! More than twice as expensive as any others.

"Lucky you," said the shop manager. "Those are the very best. They can be reused forever. Just erase them, and you've got all you need for all the programs you can write."

Just erase them. But he kept getting the E R A S U R E P R O H I B I T E D message. He went through the routines in the manual, meticulously, checking every step, and still the message came up.

Oddly, it was only after hours and hours of struggle to erase that he thought of loading the used discs, and seeing what was on them, so carefully protected. F I L E S L O C K E D.   A C C E S S   P R O H I B I T E D said the screen.

Robert swore. Then he went downstairs to the kitchen and made himself a large stack of sandwiches, and put them on a tray together with the electric kettle and the jar of instant coffee, and a bottle of lumpy milk, and settled down grimly with these supplies to do battle with the devilment of the previous owner of the machine. After some time he got a new message on the screen. It now read A C C E S S   C O D E ?   The little green dot bleeped at him, waiting. If you knew the code, you typed it in, and then the thing let you read the disc. The chance of guessing the code was zero.

A disassembler. Perhaps with a disassembler he could break the code, or read it rather, finding it in the intricacies of the program. . . .

He bought a disassembler with the last of the holiday money his parents had left him, and ate two large meals from the freezer, to stock up on. Somehow he had gone off sandwiches. There weren't any clean socks left in his drawer. He put on a pair of sandals, and when that left his toes freezing, he brought the electric heater from the spare bedroom and beamed it at his feet. He was good at computers. Very good. But this was a pig of a task. More days. In desperation he read one of his mother's postcards, ran the washing machine, and put on clean socks, damp.

And then at last he got there. The code was R R T 8 4 1. Odd, that. His own initials, Robert Randall Thompson, and the date—'84, and 1. Rubbish. Coincidence. ''All this living alone is driving you loopy, Robert lad,'' he told himself, and typed. A C C E S S   C O D E? said the screen.

Triumphant, Robert typed in R R T 8 4 1.

On the front of the disc drive, the little red light lit up, and the machine purred quietly. He'd got it!

Got what, exactly?

He'd got a message that said, D I S - C O N N E C T   V D U.   C O N N E C T   T E L E V I S I O N. Nothing he did would remove this silly message, or persuade the machine to disgorge more of whatever was on the disc.

In the end, in desperation, he did it, using the small portable TV from the ironing room. His mother hated ironing, and television, but somehow found them more bearable both together.

He set the TV down, and plugged it in. At once the screen faded out the **CONNECT TV** message, and said, **AT LAST. I THOUGHT YOU'D NEVER MAKE IT. WELL, OBVIOUSLY, I KNEW YOU WOULD EVENTUALLY, BUT IT DID TAKE YOU LONG ENOUGH!**

Robert looked at this message for a long time. It made a nasty prickling sensation run down his spine. It certainly didn't look like any other computer message he had ever seen.

After a while it blipped off. He felt a momentary deep relief, and began to convince himself that damp socks and bad eating caused delusions in post–glandular-fever sufferers, when the screen came up with another line. **FOLLOW DIRECTIONS ON DISC.**

The chill returned. Robert thought deeply, and typed in, "I am not who you think I am. Previous owner of machine gone away."

The screen said **YOU ARE WHO I THINK YOU ARE. FOLLOW DIRECTIONS ON DISC.**

Robert typed in "No."

The screen showed **BUT I KNOW THAT YOU WILL. WHEN YOU ARE READY, TYPE ''CHAIN SHOPPING LIST''. THE DISC**

WILL SHOW YOU WHAT YOU ARE TO BUY.

Robert switched everything off, and went for a walk. But the message reappeared when he switched on again. He could rid himself of it easily enough, by using the VDU instead of the TV so he could settle down to his bridge program, but of course the mysterious message nagged away at the back of his mind and eventually he gave in, and typed ''CHAIN SHOPPING LIST''.

Purring, the disc drive showed him a list of computers. Model numbers, brand names. More or less everything on the market in the way of micro-computers. Some of the items had BOUGHT AND SHIPPED against them. At the foot of the list, when the machine scrolled down to it, it said, BUY ALL ITEMS NOT MARKED BOUGHT AND SHIPPED.

Robert typed in, in a fury, "Don't be bloody ridiculous, I can't buy all that stuff!"

WHY NOT? said the screen instantly.

"No money" typed Robert.

OPEN A BANK ACCOUNT said the screen.

Rage shook him. He was hating this; hating being bossed about in this ridiculous way, hating himself for not being able just to switch off and ignore it. But one reason why his mother hated television was that neither Robert nor his father could ever bring themselves to switch off lousy programs. . . .

Seething, he typed in, "I'm too young. I can't do that."

The screen answered so fast it took his breath away: YOU WILL FIND THAT YOU CAN.

And of course, he did find that he could. He told the bank manager an elaborate fairy story about being alone in the house, about some bill needing paying urgently, and his father being about to put a check in the post, and how he, Robert, would need a deposit slip to make the deposit, and a checkbook of his own to pay the bill. . . .

The bank manager was amused. "There are easier ways of doing this, you know," he said. "I'm surprised at your father. But perhaps he'd like you to get used to banking early. Most people leave it till they have to handle student grants. But we like to get customers young. Just let me know if I can help in any way; if the letter with the check doesn't arrive promptly, or anything. How much money are you putting in now?"

"Now?" said Robert, alarmed. "I haven't got any till my dad sends this check. . . ."

"Well, it isn't usual to start a bank account with absolutely nothing," the manager said.

"I've got fifty pence," said Robert.

"Great oaks from little acorns grow," said the manager cheerfully.

He was quite right, too. When, three days later, Robert used his new card to request his bank balance from the automatic till, under instruction, of course, from the inexorable screen, the balance shown was £100,000.50.

It was fun, in a way, marching into computer shops buying wildly expensive things. They kept ringing the bank to check the money, and seemed very respectful when they came back. Just the same, he began to worry that all this activity might draw attention to his account, so he withdrew a huge amount in cash, remarking to the desk clerk that his father needed it to pay builders, and began to pay cash for things. He listed into the computer what he bought. The boxes piled up in the sitting room. And the screen talked to him. It said **ZAPPO!** when he got some prized item on the list. Sometimes he couldn't get what it wanted, the listed models were superseded, and he had to ask for further instructions. Once he couldn't get the right thing, because the code number was too high; the computer listed a Diogenes 800, and the shop said it didn't exist. There were only two Diogenes micros: 50 and 100.

EVEN BETTER said the screen. **BUY THE EARLIER MODEL.** Odd, that.

Robert began to talk back a bit to the screen. "Whoever wants all this stuff?" he asked it. "Nobody uses all this. It isn't compatible. You choose one system and get only what goes with it."

I AM A COLLECTOR said the screen.

"Nobody collects computers," said Robert.

I DO said the screen. **I HAVE LOVED THEM EVER SINCE MY FATHER BOUGHT ME ONE OF THOSE FIRST MODELS WHEN I WAS A KID.**

The day came when Robert had to put a box in the hall, there being no room left in the sitting room. He wondered what his mother would say if she saw the mess, and then he looked at the calendar, and realized it was only three days till his parents came back. He bolted up the stairs, and asked the computer how to start shipping the stuff.

THAT'S THE BEAUTY OF IT said the screen.

IT ISN'T A PROBLEM. YOU JUST KEEP THE STUFF.

Keep it? Oh, gods . . .

"Impossible. Awaiting further instructions" he typed.

AS ABOVE said the screen.

"Look, what happened to the stuff the other guy bought before he quit? Can't we do the same with all this?"

THE PREVIOUS PURCHASE AGENT GOT TOO CLEVER said the screen. HE GOT HIMSELF SHIPPED WITH HIS LAST CONSIGNMENT. YOU CAN'T IMAGINE THE TROUBLE IT CAUSED. DON'T EVEN THINK ABOUT IT.

"I think it's time you came clean with me" typed Robert. "Exactly where is all this stuff going?"

NO MARKS FOR GUESSES. NOT WHERE, WHEN. THE PREVIOUS AGENT GOT OVER-EXCITED ABOUT IT. I HAD IT ALL SET UP NICELY: A SYSTEM FOR SHIPPING ANTIQUES FROM YOUR TIME HORIZON TO OURS AND THE IDIOT CRATED HIMSELF UP WITH A LOAD OF IBMS AND CAME TOO. THE BUREAUCRATS WERE OUTRAGED. HE JUST DISAPPEARED THEN AND ARRIVED NOW WITH NO PAPERS, NO PAST, NO CLUE HOW TO BEHAVE, NO MONEY. . . . THEY HAVE ABSOLUTELY FORBIDDEN FURTHER SHIPMENTS. I WAS DISMAYED. THEN I THOUGHT OF YOU. PERFECT. NO SHIPPING NEEDED. YOU JUST KEEP THE STUFF.

"But I can't!" typed Robert. "There isn't anywhere!"

ALL WORKED OUT. PUT IT STACKED CLOSELY ON THE BOARDED PART OF THE ROOF SPACE, BEHIND THE COLD WATER TANK. COVER WITH BLACK POLYTHENE SHEETING AND STRING. TIED DOWN AS IF ANOTHER TANK. THEN FORGET ABOUT IT.

"And someday I meet you? Is that it? You're crazy. What if we move? What if I die young? What if I won't part with the stuff when you suddenly turn up and ask for it?"

YOUR QUESTION A said the screen. YOU DO NOT MOVE HOUSE. YOUR QUESTION B YOU DO NOT DIE YOUNG, THAT I DO KNOW. YOUR QUESTION C NO PROBLEM. YOU STILL HAVE NOT APPRECIATED THE BEAUTY OF THIS ARRANGEMENT.

"I certainly haven't!" typed Robert. "What the hell do you mean about antiques?"

ANTIQUE EARLY COMPUTERS IN MINT CONDITION said the screen. PURE AND PERFECT DELIGHT. THERE WERE SO MANY KINDS IN THE EARLY DAYS. YOU DO NOT FOLLOW? THINK ABOUT LOOPS.

Robert did think about loops. He thought about them while he heaved and stacked boxes; while he struggled with the loft ladder, and polythene sheeting, and string; while he lay in the bath soaking off the dirt of the roof space, and the deathly weariness that the heaving brought on; well, he was supposed to be resting after glandular fever. . . . He thought about them while he chased more knowledge through the user manual, and the disassembler program. . . .

His kit was networked in some crazy way. Networked into the future computer that gave the orders. With some ingenuity, he extracted from his disc a code for user directory, and from the directory the locking code for the user issuing the purchase list. It was RRT20491. Robert Randall Thompson, in two thousand and forty nine, no doubt! Of course the shipping would be no problem; the bossy purchaser was himself, grown old in fiendish ingenuity. If he kept the things, he would own the things . . . a unique collection of antique computers in mint condition!

But what about that figure 1? What was that doing? Robert learned about loops. The computer could be sent around and around loops in the program; it could count the number of times it went around them. The 1 meant it was going around for the first time, but the very presence of a number meant it was going to go around more than once. . . .

It mustn't. He couldn't bear it. He set his tired wits at the problem again. This particular thing wasn't difficult. The computer was set for six loops. They were nested; if he touched a computer again it would find him when he was twenty-four, thirty-two, forty . . . Each time the loop was shorter, one inside another. . .

He found the program line that counted the loops. Easy. This would be easy. He inserted a line. "If n is greater than 1, endprocedure" he wrote. And then, "run."

The screen cleared. He had wiped out the loop, and

the program with it. The house seemed suddenly empty again, and full of relief.

He waited for his parents to come home before he investigated. Somehow their being around made him feel safer. He found he had a bank account with 50 pence in it. Oh, well, that would be handy when it came to student grants. There was still a pile of kit in the attic, behind the tank. He wondered if he should drag it all downstairs again sometime, and dump it in the river. . . .

Then he thought, he's incredibly ancient by 2049. He's probably long past girls and drink, and any kind of fun. If the micros give the poor old geezer pleasure, where's the harm?

So he left the stuff exactly where it was.